THE DISGRACE OF

Kitty Grey

Also by Mary Hooper

Historical fiction

At the Sign of the Sugared Plum
Petals in the Ashes
The Fever and the Flame
(a special omnibus edition of the two books above)
The Remarkable Life and Times of Eliza Rose
At the House of the Magician
By Royal Command
The Betrayal
Fallen Grace
Velvet

Contemporary fiction

Megan
Megan 2
Megan 3
Holly
Amy
Chelsea and Astra: Two Sides of the Story
Zara

THE DISGRACE OF

Kitty Grey

MARY HOOPER

BLOOMSBURY
LONDON   NEW DELHI   NEW YORK   SYDNEY

Bloomsbury Publishing, London, New Delhi, New York and Sydney

First published in Great Britain in May 2013 by Bloomsbury Publishing Plc
50 Bedford Square, London WC1B 3DP

Text copyright © Mary Hooper 2013

The moral right of the author has been asserted

A CIP catalogue record for this book is available from the British Library

ISBN 978 1 4088 2761 1

MIX
Paper from
responsible sources
FSC® C020471

Typeset by Hewer Text UK Ltd, Edinburgh
Printed and bound in Great Britain by CPI Group (UK) Ltd, Croydon CR0 4YY

1 3 5 7 9 10 8 6 4 2

www.bloomsbury.com
www.maryhooper.co.uk

Contents

Chapter One

S uddenly nervous about why the two young ladies had asked to meet me in secret, I hurried through the kitchens, went up the servants' stairs and stood waiting in the hallway between the drawing room and the front parlour, just as Miss Sophia and Miss Alice had requested.

I checked my nails, smoothed down my pinafore and sniffed. I was not used to being right inside the house and the air seemed to close about me stiflingly; an *inside* sort of air, stuffy and tickling my nose, a mixture of the previous night's coal fires, the fibres of the thick wool carpets and the scent from the bowl of dried rose petals on the hall table.

I looked at my reflection in the glass of the nearest portrait and tucked a few wayward strands of hair under my cap. Lady Cecilia was known to be a stickler for cleanliness, especially in the dairy, and I couldn't help but be worried that there had been a complaint against me. But then surely Milady would have asked Mrs Bonny, the housekeeper, to tick me off, rather than delegate the reprimand to Miss Sophia and Miss Alice, who (not just from my own observances but according to kitchen gossip) had little else in their heads but handsome young gentlemen, ballgowns and supper dances.

I sniffed again and wished for them to hurry themselves so that I might learn my fate, whatever that was. I gazed down the hall; from where I was standing I could see right up to the double front doors one way and back the other to the little room (I had heard Lady Cecilia call it a *petit salon*) where she took tea at precisely four o'clock every afternoon. All along the walls of the passageway, placed at the same distance from each other, were portraits of the family. These were mostly gloomy-brown old things, starting with Lord Baysmith the Army Major, stuffed into tight red dress uniform outside the salon door, down to Miss Sophia and Miss Alice (lighter, brighter) in blue dresses with white sashes. Directly opposite the Misses was an oil portrait of their older brother, the present Lord Baysmith's son and heir, Peregrine, who was away at school.

I counted the portraits: fourteen in all, going back years and years and depicting all the notable Bridgeford Hall residents. There was, I knew, a much more recent portrait of the present Lord Baysmith with Lady Cecilia, dressed as if for a ball but, strangely, sitting under a tree on the estate with two enormous hunting dogs borrowed for the occasion. It had been painted, apparently, by someone very famous, and now hung over the fireplace in what they called the *grand salon*. I had only seen this painting a few times but I liked it very much, for in the background the sun could be seen glinting on the river, far away, and upon this river my sweetheart, Will, worked as a ferryman. The painting showed, faintly, a rowing boat with (I had convinced myself) a smudged representation of Will inside, his strong brown arms pulling at the oars.

I slipped into a little reverie, smiling to myself as I thought of Will. We had been walking out together secretly for some months now, and the time was coming when he must call on Mrs Bonny and Mr Griffin the butler with a request that we be allowed to see each other formally. This would mean that we could meet openly after church on a Sunday or, if the ferry business was quiet, stroll to the village on a summer's evening. After we had been granted permission and walked out together for several years, we might be able to wed, providing my family were in agreement and we had somewhere to live. I was hoping that he might speak to Mrs Bonny soon – and I'd dropped plenty of hints that he should – but he was very much a waterman by trade and by type (that is, he did not give a stick for convention). Moreover, I was slightly worried that, not being aware of social pitfalls, he might say the wrong thing at the wrong time and spoil our chances.

Miss Sophia and Miss Alice suddenly came through the drawing-room door, giggling together. Miss Sophia looked at me, put her finger to her mouth to indicate I should not speak, then said in a low voice, 'Is there anyone around, Kitty?' (I should say here that although I was born Katherine, everyone in the house called me Kitty, as Katherine had been thought too much of a name for a milkmaid.)

I bobbed a curtsey. 'No, miss. Everyone's about their duties.'

'I don't mean servants! I mean family.'

I shook my head. 'I haven't seen anyone.' How would *I* see anyone, I thought, unless they came into the dairy? 'Your mother is still abed, I believe,' I added. I knew this because I'd passed through the kitchens and heard one of the upstairs maids complaining that she couldn't get into Milady's room to lay the fire and it was going to set her back for the entire day.

'Because we've got something secret to do,' said Miss Sophia. 'Something we want you to assist us with.'

I couldn't help but be surprised at this, for unless they wanted to know how to churn butter or separate the whey, there was surely nothing in the world that I knew which they didn't, what with their governesses and their riding master, their deportment lessons, their needlework and their art classes.

'And you mustn't tell a soul about it!' Miss Alice said. 'Unless you absolutely have to tell Mrs Bonny, that is.'

'Nor would I, miss,' I said earnestly (but not truthfully, for I was already concocting a story for the servants' hall).

4

'You know it is the first of May on Saturday . . .' began Miss Sophia.

I nodded, for of course every last servant in the hall had been talking about this date, their afternoon off, where they were going and what they would wear.

'Well, our mother is hosting a musical evening with poetry and so on, and Alice and I want to do something rather special.' She began giggling again; she was a giddy goat, much worse than her sister.

'Oh, honestly, Sophia!' Miss Alice frowned at her. 'Kitty, it is this: we are planning to present to the assembled company what is called a *tableau vivant*.'

I recognised that these were foreign words, for they were uttered in the strange way that Milady said *petit salon*, but they meant absolutely nothing to me.

'Silly! She won't understand that,' said Miss Sophia. 'Kitty, it means . . . it's like a still life picture. Art come to life.' She looked around the hall and pointed to an oil painting of an ancient Baysmith aunt handing a basket of provisions to a poor family, all of whom were looking up at her with grateful eyes. 'We could replicate this painting, for example: all dress up in costume and take a part.'

'But we won't do that, because we want to be milkmaids!' said Miss Alice.

'We'll be hidden behind screens, you see, frozen into graceful attitudes,' Sophia went on, adopting a pose like a ballerina, 'and then when the music finishes the screens will be taken away and everyone will be *terribly* surprised and applaud us.'

I did not ask the obvious question: Why? Why should anyone want to do such a thing?

'It's quite the latest fashion in London,' said Miss Sophia, as if guessing my thoughts.

'And we are keen that our guests should be charmed!'

'It will be an excellent amusement.'

'Yes, it will, miss,' I lied, thinking that I had never heard anything so daft in all my life – barring when our chickens at home had lost their feathers and my ma had knitted them waistcoats.

'And this is where you come in, Kitty,' said Miss Alice. 'We are going to present a *tableau* showing milkmaids in a pastoral setting. Miss Sophia and I are to play the two milkmaids, of course, and we are having new white muslin frocks run up by the dressmaker.'

'With matching bonnets,' added her sister.

'Very nice, miss,' I said, thinking that white muslin frocks would be completely foolish and impractical for a milkmaid and that the two young ladies would look much more realistic in brown cotton smocks. Maybe not quite so picturesque, though.

'One of the gardeners is making us garlands of flowers to wear.'

I looked at them blankly.

'They say that the milkmaids in London dance down the street garlanded with flowers!' Miss Alice explained.

'I see,' I said. Miss Alice was a bit of a bookworm, so she was probably right. It seemed a strange thing to do, however, even in London. Were the cows in the procession, too? Did they go first or bring up the rear? Did the cows join in the dancing?

'So, we intend to get into our places behind screens in the music room, and ask the musicians to finish their performance with something suitably pastoral,' said Miss Sophia. 'When the screens are removed there we will be, as pretty as a picture, with trees and flowers and perhaps a lamb or two.'

'And milk churns and most definitely a cow, of course.'

'A cow in the music room, miss?' I asked incredulously.

'Just one nice cow. A pretty one with long eyelashes. The reason we asked you here, Kitty, is we want you to choose one and prepare it –'

'Train it,' put in her sister.

'And then bring it into the music room secretly, through the servants' quarters.'

'I see, miss,' I said slowly, seeing the dangers in this undertaking. 'But what do you think your parents . . . what do you think Lord and Lady Baysmith will have to say about it?'

'Oh, Father will be charmed!' said Miss Alice.

'And everyone present will be so enthralled that our mother will end up being charmed, too,' added Miss Sophia.

'And will either of you be milking the cow?' I asked. *Tableau vivant*, I said to myself, just in case I forgot the words. *Tableau vivant.*

'Oh no!' Miss Sophia said in horror. 'I should be too frightened in case it kicked me.'

'Certainly we will not milk it,' added Miss Alice. 'We just intend to stand there looking quaint under a bower.'

'The gentlemen will love it!' cried Miss Sophia. She smiled at me. 'So if you would begin preparing the cow, Kitty. Perhaps you can get it used to standing about and walking to heel and so on.'

'And wearing ribbands and flowers!'

'I don't know if . . .'

Both young ladies looked at me keenly.

'We are relying on you, Kitty, to help make the evening a memorable one. There will be certain young gentlemen in the audience who we are hoping to impress,' said Miss Alice.

I bobbed a curtsey. 'I'll do my best, miss,' I said, thinking that on this occasion my best probably wouldn't be nearly good enough.

Chapter Two

Mrs Bonny came into the dairy later that afternoon to check that everything was scoured and spotless for the second milking. It was, of course, for I loved my job and did it meticulously, knowing that I was very lucky to be working at Bridgeford Hall. This employment had come about because my ma was of an age with Mrs Bonny; they'd gone to dame school together and learned their alphabet from the same primer.

At home Ma had taught me how to look after the chickens and the family cow and make butter and so on, and when I was coming up to eleven years old and looking for a position, had had the idea of sending me to Mrs Bonny with a note saying she would be pleased to renew their acquaintance and recommending me as reliable and sensible. I had started off at the hall as a kitchenmaid, helping the elderly dairymaid who'd been there, and when she left I happily took over her position.

The dairy at Bridgeford Hall was called by Lord Baysmith a *model* dairy. That was not to say that it was in miniature, but was an ideal model upon which other dairies should be based. Milord owned three great swathes of land given over to dairy farming, but my little dairy was attached to the big house, and the milk and its products (cream, butter and cheeses) from its cows were made only for the inhabitants of the household. Twice every day I washed the floor, scrubbed the marble worktops, scoured the pails and scalded and aired the pans, and when I'd milked the cows I was free to make any other dairy products needed that day.

The dairy was a round room next to the kitchens but separated from it by an airy walkway which led on to a cheese-making room and then on to a small milking parlour with stalls for four cows. The dairy, to my mind, was the nicest part of the whole house, for it had blue-veined marble worktops, white porcelain tiles, bunches of fresh mint and thyme to discourage the flies, and little water fountains to cool the air in summer and keep everything fresh. It was separate from the dairy farm next door – that big, smelly, muddy affair with lines of milking sheds – but if there was a special happening at Bridgeford, a ball or great dinner, then we would go next door in order to obtain enough cream for our flummeries and fools.

My cows were four lovely South Devons who lived in the fields just outside and got brought into the milking parlour twice a day. I thought of them as being amongst the most fortunate of animals, for they had several small pastures which they visited in rotation and, if they wished, could feed all day on lush grass and clover. They had a much better time of it than the herds of ordinary black-and-white Friesians at the big farm who gnawed the grass in their paddock until 'twas almost bald and then trampled the ground to slush. Beside them, my South Devons were very handsome beasts, more docile, and seemed to have nicer habits. They were the colour of the rich red soil and named Daisy, Buttercup, Clover and Rose. They were let out to run with a bull of the same breed once a year, after which they sometimes went into calf. Their calves usually joined the big herd, and Daisy or whoever would come back to give milk for another year. There were always four cows and they always took these names and, when one went to slaughter, another took its place. I loved them dearly but didn't weep when I lost one, because I knew I'd get just as attached to the next in line, and that that was the way of the world.

I thought it best to tell Mrs Bonny that I would not be in the dairy very much that afternoon. 'I have to take one of the cows for a walk,' I explained, hiding a smile.

'Yes, and after that I suppose you'll take one of the sheep for a ride in the carriage,' she replied sharply.

'No. Really, Mrs Bonny. I saw Miss Alice and Miss Sophia earlier and they said . . .' I lowered my voice and whispered the rest, and when I got to the *tableau vivant* business I hoped she wouldn't know what it meant so I could have the pleasure of explaining the term to her, but she did.

'Attitudes!' she said. 'Young women standing about pretending to be paintings or acting out lines of poesy. Heavens above! I didn't think it would ever reach Devonshire.'

I nodded. 'I have to get a cow used to obeying instructions, and on the first of May it has to be taken into the music room and hidden behind a screen.'

'Whatever will Society think of next?' Mrs Bonny flapped her hands in the air as if trying to dispel the very idea of a cow. 'I don't want to know. You must do what the young ladies ask – but don't tell me about it. If Lady Cecilia asks questions afterwards I want to be able to say that I knew nothing.'

'So, may I go now and begin its . . . training?'

She gave a nod, then changed it to a shake of her head. 'Oh, I don't know, I'm sure.'

I went.

Agreeable though my work was, I was also very happy to have a reason for escaping it and taking a walk with one of the cows, for that gave me the perfect excuse to go down to the river and see Will.

He laughed to see me leading Daisy on a rope, but looked almost indignant when I told him the reason for it and the lengths the Misses were going to for a few minutes' entertainment.

''Tis called a . . . a *tableau vivant*,' I said carefully, trying to remember the shape Miss Alice's lips had made when she'd said those words.

'No matter what they call it, 'tis not right. Your young

12

ladies are to have gowns and bonnets made especially to play-act? Not to keep them warm or dry, but to wear for only a few minutes and then discard?'

I found myself defending them. 'If they wish to, why not? They are a wealthy family and may surely do whatever they like with their money.'

'But is it proper that they should scatter it on frivolities when so many are starving?'

'The dressmaker will be pleased; she'll profit from it,' I pointed out. 'And the draper and milliner.'

It was very like Will to wax indignant like this. He'd not had an easy life, I knew; he'd helped his father on the ferry since he was nine or ten, but when he was fourteen his father had died, leaving him in charge of both the rowing boat and his youngest sister, Betsy (for his ma had died in childbed). Betsy had gone to live with their older sister, Kate, and Will had come to live in the ferryman's shelter at the river's edge. His new home was little more than a few planks of wood, chill and bare, but it meant he was always there, ready and available to ferry people across the river for a penny each way.

Just then, protesting about the Misses' gowns, he looked so handsome, with his eyes so blue in his tanned-by-the-wind face, that I could not help but smile at him.

'Don't let's argue,' I said. 'I see little enough of you that we should have cross words about something so silly – something that is nothing to do with either of us but only concerns lords and ladies.'

He frowned still and I made a face at him, and after a moment his mood changed, and he smiled, caught hold of my free hand and kissed it. I believe he would have kissed me on the lips then – and I was willing enough – but we heard a cry of 'Will! Oh, Will!' from further along the river and turned to see Betsy running through the trees from the direction of the village.

Now, I loved Betsy as if she were my own little sister, but I have to say that my heart sank on seeing her, for I hardly ever got time on my own with Will. Although Betsy had lived with Kate and her husband for three years, the couple had four young children of their own and not much time to bother about an extra one. Consequently, Betsy doted on Will (and he on her) and she spent most of her waking hours with him down by the river, splashing through the reeds, chasing insects to feed to the frogs, climbing trees and playing house.

She reached us and Will picked her up and swung her round. When he'd put her down and she'd caught her breath, her first question was to ask why I had a cow with me.

'I've got Daisy in tow because I'm training her,' I explained. 'She's going to be acting in a play and I have to teach her how to behave herself, how to walk daintily and come to me when I call.'

'A play?' She frowned at me. 'What? Like in church at Easter?'

'Something like that,' I said. 'You can help me get her ready, if you like. You can walk her up and down along the riverbank and . . .' I tried to think of what else an obedient cow would do, '. . . get her to answer to her name.'

Betsy looked from me to Will. She was scarce five years old but she knew that I was trying to be rid of her.

'It's for Miss Sophia and Miss Alice,' I said persuasively, for although Betsy had only ever viewed these two young ladies from afar, I knew she very much admired their gowns, their hair and their fashionable demeanour. Quite often, when the Misses went down the drive in their smart little carriage with parasols aloft, I saw Betsy peeping over the wall at them.

'Is it really for them?' she asked breathlessly.

'Honestly and truly.' I crossed my fingers and added, 'And Miss Sophia asked especially that Miss Betsy Villiers should help in the training of Daisy.'

Betsy fell for it and, taking the rope from me, she marched off with Daisy. When she got to the trees we heard her say, 'Daisy! We're going to walk along here and when I say *Stop!* you must be a good cow and stop walking.'

Laughing, Will and I went to sit in his rowing boat and, after we'd shared a kiss or two, he started talking about the subject he lately held most dear to his heart: London. Where, apparently, the streets were paved with gold and every man could live like a king.

'The watermen on the Thames earn four pence a trip and there are always customers. It's possible to earn ten

15

shillings a day. A day!' he repeated. 'If I saved I'd soon have enough money to buy a little cottage.'

'What am I supposed to do while you're off in London earning all this money?' I asked. I looked at him coyly. 'And what if I have my head turned by a visiting peddler or a lad at the Friday market?'

'You wouldn't be here to have your head turned – you'd be by my side. You'd have to come to London with me.'

'To London? What would a milkmaid do in London? 'Tis all gin shops, taverns and coffee houses.'

'For certain it is not!' he said. 'People live in houses there, just as they do here. And where there are people there are servants – and milkmaids. You'll easily find employment.'

I shook my head. 'I don't think I'd like it there,' I said. 'I've seen pictures . . . there are robbers and footpads and a deal of noise and clamour. People get knocked over in the streets and mown down by horses. Besides, I'd never see my family.'

'You hardly see them now,' he pointed out, which was true, for although my mother and father were only ten miles off in Arlington, it was too far to walk there and back on my day off and near impossible to get a lift on a cart. Carts went to market, and to the next village, but there was no reason for anyone to go to Arlington. 'We'd only need to stay there a year or so,' he said. A strand of hair had escaped from my cap and he took it up and twirled it around his finger.

'Just think, Kitty, one year in London and then we could be wed.'

I sighed. I had to own that it was a tempting thought.

'Whereas if I stay here, the Lord knows how long it will take to get a proper roof over our heads. I know I could not ask you to . . .' He gestured behind him towards the hut.

I answered quickly with a disgusted 'No, for certain you could not!'

'It might be ten years. Do you really want to wait ten years for me?' he asked, his fingers encircling my wrist.

'But they say London is a wicked place . . .'

'We'd be together. I'd protect you from all wickednesses!'

'But where would we live if I ever agreed to go? Which I certainly don't,' I added hastily.

'We could live with my cousins,' he said. 'They're watermen born and bred and they live –'

'Near the Cathedral of St Paul's,' I said, for I had heard about these blessed relations regularly. 'I know all about them! They can see the very dome of it from their window.'

'So they can,' he said, laughing.

'But what about Betsy? She'd miss you terribly.'

'She'd stay safe at home with Kate, and we'd send her toys and sweetmeats from London. And we'd soon be back here and then she could come and live with us in our own cottage. After we're wed, of course,' he added, seeing the look of pretended affront on my face. His

17

hand ran up my arm. 'Come with me, Kitty. Let's be together in London . . .'

'I'll think about it,' I said, for although I did not intend to do any such thing and the thought of London rather scared me, I didn't want him to know this, or to stop trying to persuade me.

I believe there would have been some more kisses following this, but our tryst was interrupted then by a call of 'Halloo!' from the opposite bank of the river, and I jumped out of the boat and let Will row across and pick up the two men who were waiting to be brought over. I rescued Daisy from Betsy and she and I together fashioned a headdress for the cow made of willow-weed, rushes and kingcups, which suited the big, handsome animal very well. I assured Betsy that I would tell Miss Alice and Miss Sophia that she'd had a hand in the making of it, then made my way back to the big house, wondering all the way what would happen to us, to me and Will, if I didn't go with him to London. I didn't *think* he'd go without me – but I wasn't keen to put this notion to the test.

Chapter Three

The first day of May arrived and it was impossible to say whether or not Daisy was trained. Sometimes she was, and sometimes she wasn't. I loved all my cows, but I thought this particular one was perhaps the most agreeable: clean, sensible, dreamy, limpid-eyed. She was also reasonably regular in her habits, which made it possible to judge when she might open her bowels. This was particularly important if Daisy was not to bring disgrace to us all on the music-room floor.

Miss Sophia and Miss Alice had visited the dairy several times (the model dairy, of course, not the real, stinking muddy place) in order to acquaint themselves with such necessities as milking buckets, butter scales, cream-setting pans and so on. It really would not do, I told them as respectfully as possible, to be seen holding a milking bucket at the wrong end of a cow, for although they were not actually going to milk it on stage ('Oh, perish the thought!' Miss Sophia had said), they should at least look as if they knew one end of a cow from the other.

The milkmaids' dresses were finished and I had been allowed to have a peep at them. They were of white silk rather than muslin and very pretty indeed, being in the newly fashionable high-waisted style with lace across the bosom and pink ribbands unfurling down the front. They were clearly completely impractical for a dairy-maid; in real life the flouncing around the hem would be stiff with mud and the pink ribbands would trail into the milking bucket in no time at all, but I didn't say this. I had already worked out for myself that it was the *idea* of the pastoral life that was important, not the actuality. The Misses' hair was to be dressed in ringlets for the occasion (as if I ever had the time to wear my own hair so!) over which they would not wear bonnets now, but ruffled mob caps in silk to match their dresses.

On the first of May, everyone was in a gay mood, for most of the servants had been granted the afternoon off to go into the village and enjoy the festivities. Our hamlet was not large enough to be visited by a travelling fair, but the church was to be decorated with flowers, there would be peddlers selling sweetmeats and toys, a maypole had been erected on the green and morris men were to dance. Because we were taking the afternoon off, however, all our work had to be done in the morning, so there were chamber pots to be emptied, beds to be made, fireplaces to be cleaned out, meals to be cooked and (in my case) cows to be milked and butter churned, before we could make merry. Consequently, we were all out of bed that morning at three o'clock, trying to get as much work out of the way as possible before breakfast.

But there was another, much more pleasant duty to be undertaken that morning, and at seven o'clock, our most arduous chores completed, we gathered by the door to the kitchen garden in order to go into the fields and wash ourselves in morning dew, for it was said that doing this on May Day morning would make a girl beautiful. Most of the female servants of the hall were waiting there, whether or not they believed this to be true – even those well past the first flush of youth whom you might have imagined had stopped caring about such things. I went, too, of course, even though I'd been working at the hall for four May Days now and had never seen any changes in anyone after we'd washed, either in the mirror or in one of my fellow servants becoming suddenly more beautiful.

I noticed that Faith, Miss Alice's maid, did not come to wait by the door but carried on making up a tray for her mistress's breakfast.

'Are you not joining us?' I asked.

She shook her head. 'But I shall accompany Miss Alice and Miss Sophia when they go out in the carriage a little later.'

'They are going out for the May dew?' I asked, and she nodded, while I thought how unjust it would be if either

21

of these young ladies, after bathing in dew, were to be transformed into radiant beauties. Why, they already had the very best that life could offer: the finest of gowns, money, an education and a personal maid! If they became beautiful (instead of merely pleasant-looking), it would be annoying in the extreme.

A dozen or so of us left the house together and went past my cows and into the next field, which was lush with forget-me-nots and daisies. Laughing and calling to each other, we rolled up our sleeves and tucked our hair into our caps in readiness to splash our faces. Whilst trying to twist my long hair into a knot, I looked towards the river, hoping to see Will and give him a wave. I knew he was sure to be up and about tinkering with his boat, for there was a deal of money to be earned that day from all the people who'd be coming and going. The morris men, for example, were coming over the water from Millbridge, and there were ten persons in their set: six dancers, a fool and three musicians to be taken back and forward, five at a time. If every day were as busy as May Day, I thought wistfully, then Will would have no need to go to London to work.

Seeing him appear from his hut, I waved both arms and would have shouted if I'd been on my own. He didn't appear to be looking in our direction, but then Betsy came into view, running along the riverbank to have her breakfast with him, and she pointed in my direction so that Will saw me and waved and whis-tled.

Mrs Bonny straightened up from the grass, her face shiny with dew. 'I trust that the ferryman is not signalling to one of my girls in that vulgar manner,' she said, but I knew she was not being serious.

'Aye. 'Tis me he whistles to,' said old Ma Crocker, who comes in to do embroidery, and we all laughed.

I patted my face with water to cool it down, then taking my courage in both hands said, 'Mrs Bonny, I do believe he is waving to me, for I have spoken to him several times and . . . and we have an understanding.'

'Indeed!' Mrs Bonny arched her eyebrows.

'I think Will –'

'Oh, *Will*, is it?'

I nodded, realising she must already know his name and was teasing me. 'He – Will – intends to come to speak to you soon.'

'I should think he does. And not afore time,' she added drily. I felt myself blushing again, for I'd been told the rules about followers when I'd first started at the hall (although at eleven years old I could hardly comprehend what the term meant) and knew that Will should really have approached Mrs Bonny and Mr Griffin before now.

A few moments later the dew had dried on our arms and faces and we had covered ourselves up with our shawls and were ready to go back to the hall.

'You're a sly puss, young Kitty,' said Patience, one of the kitchenmaids, coming up close and speaking in my ear. '*Now* I know where you're going when you tell us you're putting your cows away.'

'We've only been seeing each other a few months.'

'But I can't say I blame you, keeping him to yourself. He's a good-looking lad.'

'He is,' I agreed readily.

'Bit *too* handsome, to my way of thinking.'

I should have left it at that, but couldn't help but ask what she meant.

'Why,' she answered, 'just that if I was courting a young man like that I'd never have a moment's peace. He must have girls breaking their hearts over him every day.'

'Yes, but . . .' I began. *He loves me*, I was going to say, but the words stuck. Did he love me? How would I know?

In the event, thinking about this weighty subject stopped me enjoying the May Day afternoon, because I couldn't think of anything else. If Will did love me, why hadn't he said so?

I sighed as I admired the church flowers, heaved another sigh as I watched the maypole dancing, and did not stop long enough to see the morris men perform. I resolved to speak to Will on my way back to the hall but, of course, when I got there he was much too busy with all his May Day passengers, and I had to be content with a wink and a whisper that he would see me the following morning.

Rather miserably I went home to prepare for Miss Alice and Miss Sophia's evening performance, only to discover, with ten minutes to go before Daisy's debut, that cows don't like climbing stairs.

Her route had been carefully planned: she was to climb the stone steps from the kitchens up to the hallway and from here proceed, quiet and unseen, into the dining room and through into the back of the music room, ready for the *tableau*.

All the servants were now in on the secret, for, of course, it had not been possible to prepare Daisy – that is, soap her down, ring her little horns with flowers and hang a garland around her neck – without rousing their suspicion that there was something a little odd going on. Miss Alice and Miss Sophia's personal maids, Faith and Christina, had been told of it some time ago, and had been practising not only their ringlet-making, but also applying a subtle blush of colour to their ladies' cheeks so that they looked pink and sun-kissed, as if they'd been in the fresh outdoors. Now, though, they were berating me for not training Daisy well enough.

'The very first thing you should have done, Kitty, was to try and make this cow go up steps!' Faith said as the three of us endeavoured to push Daisy's hindquarters upwards.

I did not deign to reply, though I could have asked how I was supposed to train a cow to walk up and down the kitchen stairs *in secret* when there were a dozen or more people cooking meals in the same area.

'Yes, the first and most obvious thing is the stairs,' said Christina, puffing and panting. 'Indeed, 'twas hardly necessary to teach it about anything except stairs.'

Faith paused to draw breath. 'And could you not have found a smaller cow?'

'Quite! This must be the biggest and most ungainly animal in the herd!'

I didn't reply, indignant at the insults to Daisy. Why, she was not ungainly at all – or, if she appeared so it was only in the house. And that was as it should be, for cows are not bred for drawing rooms.

It was Mrs Bonny, thank goodness, who came up with the solution. She fashioned a large sling affair from a length of sacking which had been used to bind up hay bundles and, with her at one end of it and Mr Griffin at the other, they came from behind with a '*Heyyyy-up!*' and managed to scoop Daisy who, surprised and shocked, bolted up the steps before she hardly knew what she was doing. From here, with me holding tightly to her collar, we proceeded at a tidy trot down the hallway, through the dining room and into the back of the music room. Here behind folded screens, which hid them from the rest of the room, I found Miss Alice and Miss Sophia looking exquisite in their silk gowns (but, I was pleased to see, not turned into beauties from the dew). Around them, thanks to help from the gardeners, stable hands, estate managers and goodness knows who else, the scene was set for a pastoral idyll, with a painted backcloth showing sunlit fields, flowers and a thatched cottage. The two Misses were sitting on milking stools, their gowns becomingly arranged around them and their garlands colourful, surrounded by an array of gleaming artefacts for the audience's contemplation: milk churns, enamel buckets, a cream separator and several other quaint dairy objects.

Daisy was to stand between the two girls, face on to the audience ('Whatever happens, we must not let anyone see the rear of the cow,' Miss Sophia had instructed, her face registering horror at such a thought) and, still hidden behind the screens, I turned the obliging cow around. Owing to the length of time it had taken to get her up the steps, we didn't have to wait long and, accordingly, when given the nod by Miss Sophia, I passed Daisy's flower-bedecked rope to her and slipped back into the dining room, lingering by the doorway in case of any trouble.

There was a quartet playing and when they finished I heard polite applause from the assembled audience, following which a chord was played as if the musicians were going to strike up again. At this point Miss Alice hissed loudly over the screens, 'No, you must not!'

The heir, the Honourable Peregrine, who was home from school for the occasion, addressed the audience. 'We now have a surprise for our guests,' he announced. 'My mother and father know nothing about this, but I trust they will enjoy it as much as everyone else.'

I heard a little stir in the audience as everyone turned to see how Milord and Lady Baysmith might be taking this announcement and, looking anxiously at the scene, I prayed that the Misses would not extend the performance for too long in case Daisy disgraced herself in their noble presence. I could just see Lady Cecilia from where I was standing; she was dressed regally (but not fashionably), in the old manner of hooped petticoat and crinoline, her hair powdered and teased into cascades of curls.

'My sisters, Sophia and Alice,' Peregrine declared, 'have much pleasure in presenting you with a pastoral scene: *Milkmaids at Rest.*'

As he said these last words, two of the valets stepped forward and pushed away the screens to reveal, solemn and still, Miss Alice, Miss Sophia and Miss Daisy the Cow, surrounded by pieces of false countryside.

There were some gasps, then a roar of approval and an inordinate amount of clapping, most especially from the young men in the audience. Two naval gentlemen in the back row stood on their chairs to get a better view of the Misses, for they did look very picturesque indeed, dressed as they were in pale, clinging fabric which left little to the imagination. Their pose was held for at least two minutes, gazing over the potted tree into the imaginary distance, and dear Daisy did not disgrace herself either, but stood steady and stoic, occasionally blinking and no doubt wondering where her field had gone.

Another signal was given and the men brought back the screens to hide the scene from view. Miss Alice and Miss Sophia kissed each other, looking very pleased with themselves and I waited for them to see and be pleased with *me*. Alas, before this could happen, Patience appeared in the hall, beckoning me with some urgency.

I went over.

'Coo, you're going to catch it and no mistake!' she said, not even trying to hide her glee at this notion.

'How am I?' I answered. 'I was only following orders from Miss Sophia and Miss –'

'I don't mean because of the cow and all that.'

'What, then?'

'Your sweetheart, from the ferry. He's here in the kitchens wanting to see you. Bold as brass he came, knocking on the kitchen window.'

'Will's here?' My first thought was that he had come to see Mrs Bonny and ask her permission to call on me, but then I realised it was gone nine o'clock. No one in polite company called at such an hour.

'You'd better get down to the kitchens sharpish! I'll see to the cow, if you like.'

I was torn, for I'd been looking forward to receiving the Misses' grateful thanks and perhaps a small silver coin for my trouble, but I didn't dare hesitate and went straight down to the kitchens.

Chapter Four

'He's over there,' Mrs Bonny said, nodding towards the fireplace. 'And I need not tell you of the impropriety of this, Kitty. It is most unseemly.'

'For a dairymaid to have a caller at this hour – *really*!' said Mr Griffin. 'It won't be tolerated twice, you know that.'

I curtseyed to Mr Griffin in an apologetic sort of way and hurried over to Will, who was hunched over, looking uncomfortable, holding his hat scrunched up in his hands and standing as close to the garden door as it was possible to get without actually being on the other side of it.

'You shouldn't have come!' I hissed, which I know was not very kind of me, but I could not help but be acutely embarrassed by having what seemed like every servant in the household witness this little scene.

'I had nowhere else to turn.'

'I don't understand. What do you mean?'

He shot a look at Mrs Bonny and Mr Griffin. 'Can we go outside?' he asked me in a low voice.

I nodded and pulled at the door latch.

'You've got five minutes,' Mr Griffin said. 'No longer.'

I thanked him and, as Will and I went outside, saw Daisy on her return journey from the music room, lumbering down the steps into the kitchens, followed by a grinning Patience.

Outside the garden door, there was the stub of a wax candle burning in a sconce, but the moon was hidden by cloud so it was impossible to see very far across the fields. You could hear the wind rustling the new leaves on the trees, however, and, far away, the sound of the river.

'What is it?' I asked urgently, worried now about why he was there. Was it something to do with my family? Had one of them been taken ill?

'I need to ask you something really important.'

I stared at him wonderingly. Surely he wasn't . . . ?

'It's my sister, Kate – her husband has lost his job on the Cox estate.'

'Has he?' I looked at Will, bemused. The Cox family were the other big landowners in the district and I knew Kate's husband, George, held a position as one of their stockmen. But I couldn't think what this had to do with me or Will.

'I must explain myself better.' Will glanced over to the wide, low brick wall, where I could see something that looked like a bundle of old clothes. 'George and Kate went to the May Day celebrations today,' he continued, 'and later Kate came home to put the children to bed while George stayed on with some of his fellow workers, drinking and carousing.'

I shrugged and nodded. There was nothing unusual in this.

'But old man Cox turned up and George, being drunk, took it upon himself to list the disadvantages of working for him, saying he was a miserly devil and the men on the Baysmith estate earned far more than he and his fellow workers got from Cox.'

I clapped my hand to my mouth.

'Eventually, after the name-calling, it fell to fisticuffs. George landed a hefty blow on the old man, and he tumbled back into the fireplace and knocked himself out.'

'No!'

'George went home, and the first thing old Cox did when he came to was to send the constable round to Kate and George's cottage to turn them out.' Will blew his nose, clearly upset. 'They had to borrow a hay wagon from one of the farms, load on all their possessions – and the children – and now George and my poor sister have trundled off to who-knows-where.'

'Oh!' I exclaimed. 'But what of . . . ?'

He nodded. 'Yes, Betsy.'

'Have they taken her, too?'

'That's just it. Kate said she couldn't possibly take on another child, that they had barely enough money to feed themselves and she didn't know what might happen to them. If George can't get work – and he might not be able to do that without a Character from his old employer – they'll end up in the workhouse.'

'But . . .' I tried to grasp what this might mean for Will. 'So Betsy . . . ?'

'My sister said that four children on a wagon was more than enough and she just couldn't take her.'

I was silent for a long moment, absorbing all this news, and then I asked where she was.

Will pointed to what I'd thought was the bundle of clothes on the wall. 'She's there. Asleep.'

'You've brought her *here*?'

'I couldn't think of what else to do with her,' he said with despair. 'I couldn't just abandon her, could I?' I didn't say anything to this and he went on, 'She's already had a rough time of it – no mother, her dadda dying, then having to go and live with someone who didn't really want her.'

'Other children get by,' I said, which, I own, was a very selfish and unfeeling thing to say.

'Kitty!' Will said reproachfully. 'She's my little sister.'

I immediately felt terrible. 'Sorry, Will.' My eyes filled with guilty tears. 'I didn't mean that.'

'She's five years old. Would you really have her taken into the workhouse?'

'Of course not! But I thought you were set on going to live in London. How can that happen now?'

'I can go later, when things are settled. Maybe George will apologise and he and Kate will come back here to live and –'

'So where will Betsy stay? You're surely not going to let her live in your old shed?'

He shook his head. 'What I was wondering was . . . whether Mrs Bonny would let her stay here.'

'*Here?*' I asked, shocked. 'Here at the hall?'

Will nodded. 'She wouldn't be any trouble! She can stay with me in the day – she's happy enough doing that – and at night she could just come up here and sleep in any old spot. She'd be happy in the kitchens in front of the fire.'

I didn't reply, and he went on, 'The gardeners' children run around the estate like puppies; one more in the pack would hardly be noticed.'

'I don't know if I dare ask such a thing,' I said.

'I'm fair desperate, Kitty,' Will said, taking my hand. 'It's the only thing I can think of. I can't put her in an orphanage. You wouldn't want to see that happen, would you?'

'No, but . . . but what if Kate and George don't ever come back?'

'Well, I suppose we'll be starting our married life with a ready-made family,' he said, squeezing my hand.

I managed to smile, but thought to myself that that wasn't what I'd wanted at all: I'd wanted us to live in a little cottage on our own and only then, after a year or two, say to Will that it was time that he made a rocking cradle.

'Kitty! You've gone into a dream. What do you think I should do? Should I go and ask Mrs Bonny now, or Mr Griffin – or wait until morning?'

I sighed. 'I think they'll take it better coming from me,' I said. 'I'll ask them. Betsy will have to stay the night here, at least.'

'And I'll come for her in the morning,' Will said, and kissed my forehead. 'Thank you for what you're doing. I love you.'

My heart gave a jolt at this, but I was too overwhelmed to respond.

'Milord would throw a fit!' Mrs Bonny said when I'd finished explaining and begging. 'This is a dairy farm, not an orphanage. We can't go taking in stray children willy-nilly!'

Most of the servants had gone to bed, thank goodness, although a scullery maid was there, trying to appear busy polishing the cutlery but actually listening to us for all she was worth.

I looked from Mrs Bonny to Mr Griffin imploringly. 'But the poor child . . .'

'What happened to her mother?' asked Mr Griffin.

'She died giving birth to Betsy's twin. The twin died, too,' I added, and heard a shocked intake of breath from Mrs Bonny.

'And her father?' Mr Griffin asked.

I shrugged. 'He died shortly after Betsy's ma. I'm not sure what of.'

'What work did he do?'

'He worked the ferry, Mr Griffin – had a little cottage down the lane. Will took over the rowing boat but he couldn't afford the rent on the cottage, so now he stays in the hut down by the water.'

'Couldn't the child live there with him?' Mrs Bonny asked.

I shook my head. 'That was Will's first thought, Mrs Bonny, but the place is green with damp all year round and half under water in the winter.'

Neither of them spoke for a while, but I saw them exchanging glances.

'She would be with Will all day, as she is now!' I said quickly. 'He catches enough fish for them to eat, and whenever the baker crosses the river he pays Will in bread. Betsy would not cost Lord and Lady Baysmith a penny! I'm just asking if she could sleep here at the hall, and perhaps be inside during a rainstorm.'

Their silence continued. I could supply Will and Betsy with milk, I thought, and a little cheese and a few pats of butter disappearing into the ferryman's hut would never be noticed. And it was not all bad, for Betsy would keep Will from going to London.

'Milord and Milady need not even know she is here,' I suggested tentatively.

'Certainly they must know!' Mr Griffin cut in. 'But I believe, with Milady's propensity for charitable works, and knowing the child is motherless, she might look favourably on her staying for a while, until alternative arrangements can be made. What do you think, Mrs Bonny?'

'I suppose the child could sleep in one of the haylofts, with the gardeners' and woodcutters' children,' Mrs Bonny replied.

I nodded eagerly. There was, I knew, a little row of gardeners' cottages on the estate, but these comprised only one room with a sleeping alcove, so a lot of the workers' children slept in one of the barns. Betsy would be a little younger than the others, but this was probably all to the good, for the older girls would want to mother her just as they mothered their little sisters and brothers.

'And next March when the crops come through she could do a little work,' I said. 'Perhaps she could go out as a bird-scarer in the fields.'

Mrs Bonny shook her head and frowned. 'That's nearly a whole year away. Let's hope a proper home has been found for the child by then.'

'Of course, Mrs Bonny, Mr Griffin,' I said, dropping a curtsey first to her and then the butler and saying how very grateful Will would be, and that he would be sure to take them over the river on the ferry for free whenever they wanted to go. I said I'd wake Betsy, tell her what was happening and take her over to the hayloft.

As it happened, though, I couldn't wake her up; she was in the deep, deep sleep of a child. I was feeling guilty by then because of how I'd not really wanted to take her in, and felt I couldn't just abandon her to wake up in the hayloft, so I took her to my room in the attic and tucked her in at the foot of my bed. I shared a room with Patience and her sister, Prudence, but luckily both of them were asleep by then, so I didn't have to explain anything. The morning, I thought, would be time enough for that.

As I closed my eyes on the whole day I heard the clocks in the house striking midnight. I considered what had happened and what might happen, and then I remembered that Will had told me he loved me, and that it was the first time.

Chapter Five

'Why am I here? I don't like it here . . .' This is what I heard when I woke the following morning, and opened my eyes in the semi-darkness to see Betsy at the bottom of my bed, staring over the blanket at Patience and Prudence, who were staring back at her.

'Who are they?' Betsy asked, her voice trembling.

'What's she doing here?' Patience asked.

'Where's she come from?' said Prudence.

Betsy began to cry and I bent over, lifted her up and put her in beside me. I then shot a look at the other two: an imploring, please-don't-make-this-hard look.

'Well, you know Kate and her family have had to go away for a little while?' I began, explaining it to Patience and Prudence as much as to Betsy, who carried on crying. She didn't say anything, so I continued, 'Well, they have, and they don't know yet where they're going to be living. When they do find out, I expect they'll send for you, but in the meantime, guess where you're going to live?'

But Betsy didn't want to guess. She carried on crying, while Patience and Prudence got up; one to pour water from the washing jug into the basin and the other to use the chamber pot.

I went on. 'Well, Mrs Bonny – you like Mrs Bonny, don't you, Betsy? – is going to let you stay here in the hall at night! That is, not exactly inside, but you can sleep in the hay barn with the other children. And there are lovely little field mice in the hay barn. You like mice, don't you?'

Betsy nodded and, after a moment, stopped crying.

'You could have some as pets. Dear little brown fluffy ones,' I said, hiding a shudder, for I don't like rodents, big or small. 'And in the daytime you can play down by the river with Will, just as you usually do.'

'Every day?' she asked.

'Every single day.'

'In the rain?' Prudence put in, tipping her bowl of washing water out of the window into the area below. 'Last May it rained for eighteen days solid.'

'When it rains,' I said to Betsy, 'then you can stay in the barn, if you wish, and play with the other children.'

'And will I see Miss Alice and Miss Sophia?'

'Indeed you will,' I said. 'You will glimpse them about the place, and whenever they go riding they will come close to the barn and you will see what elegant outfits they are wearing.'

There was a snort from Prudence, for neither of the maids had any truck with the Misses (although you would never know it from all the curtseying and fawning that went on whenever they appeared).

'Now, you and I will wash our hands and faces and get dressed,' I continued to Betsy. 'Then we'll go and say good morning to Mrs Bonny and Mr Griffin. After that, I'll take you across the yard so you can see all the other children and find a little corner to sleep in.'

Betsy seemed to absorb all this information – at least, she didn't start crying again. After a moment or two, however, she asked about Will.

'He's at the river with his ferry as usual,' I answered. 'And you can go down and see him whenever you like.'

'Right now?'

'As soon as you've had some breakfast,' I said. 'And if you come into my dairy I'll draw you some fresh milk straight from the cow. You can have milk from Daisy, if you like.'

Patience and Prudence were dressed now, but still staring.

'So your sweetheart has landed you with a child,' Prudence said, clearly amused.

'But not in the usual way!' her sister giggled.

'There was nothing else to be done,' I said in a low voice. 'Will is going to take care of Betsy during the day and Mrs Bonny is allowing her to sleep in the barn at night. She's no more than a bairn!' I added, hoping to draw on their sympathy. 'I hope everyone will treat her kindly.'

'Well, it's a hard life for all of us,' Prudence said briskly. 'When our pa died, Ma had our Tommy 'prenticed as a climbing boy. Up the chimneys he used to go, fast as a weevil, and he only seven years old!'

'And I started my working life when I was eight – Ma used to send me out every morning to whiten the front steps of houses,' said Patience.

'Betsy is but four!' I said, taking a year off her age.

I explained to Betsy that I had to work every single day so wouldn't be able to spend a lot of time playing with her, and after we'd visited the barn, Will arrived to collect her for the day. While he spoke very humbly and thankfully to Mrs Bonny and Mr Griffin, I got on with my milking so that I could send him and Betsy on their way with a can of still-warm milk and some of the previous day's butter.

In the days following, we got into a routine. In the mornings Betsy would go off to the river on her own, carrying a little parcel containing whatever I'd found for them to eat that day, while I stood outside the dairy, watching her running across the fields, turning every ten yards or so to wave to me. Smaller and smaller, deeper in the grass she got, until she reached the river, then she and Will would both turn and wave as a signal that she'd arrived safely. Sometimes, if the weather was bad, she would stay in the barn with the other children, but mostly she would choose to go down to the river and be with Will. In the evenings, after they had eaten, Will would either bring Betsy back to the house or, if he was busy with passengers, she would run up to me on her own.

Several weeks after she'd first come to live at the hall, something a little unusual happened. I was some distance from the house and shooing my cows down to the bottom pasture after their afternoon milking, when Miss Sophia came out of the gate to the kitchen garden, dressed very nicely in a gown of spotted muslin with a hat covered in soft veiling.

Hoping that she would be reminded that she had not yet thanked me properly for my part in the *tableau*, I made more of a fuss of the cows than usual, calling them my pretties, patting and cajoling them. When Miss Sophia approached and addressed me, I acted as if I hadn't known she was there.

'Kitty!' she said. 'Have you a moment?'

'Oh! Of course, miss,' I said, and I gave the final cow, Clover, a slap on the rear which sent her trotting through to the pasture, then shut the gate behind her.

'Can you tell me if there's a quick way to the village through here?' she asked, pointing ahead of us towards the green lane through the woods.

I nodded. 'It's likely to be rather muddy in wet weather, though, miss – and we've had rain recently,' I said, wondering why she wasn't using the gig to go to the village.

'Oh, I hadn't thought of that.' She looked down at her pretty sandals.

'Shall I run back to the house and get more suitable footwear for you, miss? I could ask Christina –'

'No!' she said very abruptly. Then she softened it to: 'No, that's quite all right, Kitty. I'm late already and I don't want to . . . to trouble anyone.'

'I see, miss,' I said, thinking it was more likely that she didn't want anyone to know that she was going out.

She flounced her gown a little. 'I'll just go along here and hope there aren't too many puddles.'

'As you wish, miss,' I said and curtseyed.

She went on her way with not a murmur of thanks nor a mention of the *tableau*, even though I'd worked so hard on getting Daisy prepared. I was to discover later that Miss had much more on her mind just then than a South Devons cow.

I looked after her, very intrigued, for usually when Miss Sophia went out it was with her sister. They would pay calls on nearby well-to-do families or visit the milliners or dressmakers, and always went in one of the carriages, open or closed according to the season. I didn't think I'd actually seen either of them walking anywhere on their own before. In my mind, their feet hardly ever touched the ground.

A week later I was even more intrigued, for Miss Sophia was out in the herb garden, next to my dairy, wearing a pale green dress with a sky-blue parasol and scarf, cutting bits and pieces from herbs with a pair of silver scissors and placing them in her trug. This activity in itself was not unusual, for both the Misses liked to work with herbs in the still room making tinctures and balms, but her outfit was unsuitable and she could hardly manage the trug because of having to juggle the parasol as well, while the scarf kept slipping off her shoulders. What was really strange, however, was that one moment I looked out from the dairy and she was there, and the next she was gone. When I went into the herb garden later all I could see was her basket containing the scissors and some sprigs of rosemary, placed out of sight beneath a clump of feverfew.

It was not until sometime later, when I had finished for the day and my pans and bowls were all scoured and scalded to perfection, that I suddenly noticed she was back in the herb garden, snipping at things and placing them in the trug as before. She'd been absent for about two hours, I realised.

I noticed nothing puzzling for several afternoons after that, for Mrs Bonny was making cheese and, this procedure needing more than one pair of hands, Patience and I were required to help her. We hardly had time for gossip, either, for the making of hard cheeses was a complicated and somewhat unreliable process and there were not many in the kitchens who had success with it.

It was Will who, a few days later, came up with another part of the puzzle concerning Miss Sophia.

Most mornings I was left to more or less my own devices. As long as there was fresh milk for the family's breakfast, and I had made enough butter and cream the day before, then my little dairy ran independently of everything else. If I stole a little time for myself after morning milking, that was my own business. This, of course, was another benefit of my ma having known Mrs Bonny, for that good lady trusted me and hardly ever interfered with what I was doing.

On this particular morning my cows had been more than usually compliant and were easily and quickly milked, so, as I had not seen Will for several days, I decided to walk down to the river with Betsy. She had adjusted remarkably quickly to her new situation and, as I had hoped, was being mothered by two little girls of eight or nine years who vied with each other as to who could baby her the most. This, it seemed to me, was as good as anyone could provide at the moment, and infinitely better than the prospects of many poor children, but would not do for ever. I felt quite sure that Kate and her husband would soon come back to the village and take Betsy off our hands.

Now she danced along beside me, talking of the field mice she was hoping to catch that day and how Will had said that living beside the river with your own ferry boat was the best job in the world.

'Does he never speak of going to London now?' I asked her.

'Oh, he does!' she replied. 'And he said you and I shall soon go, too, and we will travel in carriages when we are there, eat meat every day and have muslin dresses.'

'Do you want to go there?'

'Yes, I really do,' she answered seriously, 'because Miss Sophia and Miss Alice go there in the Season to attend dances, and we would be able to see them in their ballgowns.'

'Well, I declare there could be no better reason to go!' I said, and Will, who had jumped out of his boat to come and meet us, heard the last of this conversation and laughed.

'I have something to recount about Miss Sophia,' I said, when Will had kissed us both good morning and enquired as to how we were faring. I told him of the two incidents and asked if Miss had ever taken the ferry.

'Not she!' Will said. 'A common rowing boat wouldn't suit. If she wanted to go into town she would surely go in a carriage to Thorndyke and over the bridge. But then . . .'

'What?' I asked, much intrigued, for there had not been much in the way of gossip in the hall of late, and we did all enjoy a little tittle-tattle.

We sat down together on the grass. 'Well, twice this week I have ferried a certain person over the river from Millbridge. He was a young naval gentleman and something of a stranger to the area.'

'Never!'

'I did wonder what business he was on, to be coming over here twice.'

'And did he say anything?'

'No, but he sighed a lot and gazed towards the hall uttering lines of poesy.'

I gave a little gasp, but Will was laughing.

'No, I am teasing you! He was a very correct young man and I believe from one of the ships at Plymouth.'

'And did he go towards the hall?'

'As I recall, he went towards the hamlet – perhaps going through the wood,' Will said, 'although I can't be sure of that because I had several strangers on board that day.'

'Oh! But you should have remembered something like that!'

'I didn't realise how very important it was going to be.'

'Stop teasing!' I begged. I made sure Betsy was employed in catching minnows before I asked eagerly, 'But how old is he? Was he a handsome gentleman? Would he make a suitable husband for Miss Sophia?'

'I have no idea,' Will said. 'I am no expert on marriage. Or love.'

There was a moment's pause after he said that last word and we smiled at each other.

'On the contrary, I believe you are,' I said and, daringly, I leaned closer and kissed him.

We broke away from each other, for Betsy had become aware of the silence and had turned round to stare at us. 'Now, about our naval friend,' I continued. 'What was he like? How tall, and did he show a good leg?'

'I did not notice his leg,' Will said, laughing, 'but I believe he was an officer, judging from the number of stripes on his arm.'

'But of course!' I said suddenly. 'At the *tableau*, there were two young naval officers in the back row who stood on their seats in order to see better. Perhaps it is one of those who is paying court to Miss Sophia.'

'If he is, then old man Baysmith may not like it,' Will said, 'for he's an Army man, is he not, and they hold themselves superior to the Navy.'

'Do they?' I thought back to the night of the first of May. Could I remember any more details? Yes, there were two young men standing on the chairs cheering, and Lady Cecilia had frowned at them, most displeased at this impropriety, and I was sure I could remember Miss Sophia gazing over the heads of the audience and smiling especially sweetly at someone. But maybe that had just been my imagination.

When I went to bed that night I thought of Miss Sophia and wondered how it felt for someone in her position to be in love, and if it was any different to the way I felt about Will. I concluded that it was not: that position and money did not alter feelings, that anyone could experience love, rich or poor, and that it was an excellent thing to happen to a girl.

Chapter Six

The month of May went into June. Clover, the oldest of my cows, developed foot rot and had to be taken across to the farm and – I presumed, for I never asked about these things – slaughtered. A new Clover arrived, younger and friskier, recently calved, and her antics leaping about the field seemed to infect the other three, so that they played up whenever I needed to catch them for milking, thundering up and down the pastures, making it near impossible to get hold of them. Once they kicked a fence down and got into a field of wild garlic, and for three days their milk was tainted with it and Lord Baysmith complained. Even when I'd got them safely into the dairy they would sometimes stamp and jitter, pull away from me or even kick over the bucket of milk.

As a consequence of all the frisking around, milking took three times as long as it usually did and, often feeling cross and exasperated, I didn't have the leisure to keep a look out for Miss Sophia. The only thing that did happen concerning her was that one night in the servants' hall everyone was agog because raised voices had been heard from the drawing room and Lord Baysmith had shouted, 'Over my dead body, my girl!' in a voice which carried right down to the kitchens.

Miss Sophia's personal maid, Christina, could probably have told us more about it – and we were so desperate to know – but, of course, no one was so ill bred as to ask her.

Hearing the Lord Baysmith incident recounted, I was glad I hadn't told the others my two little stories about Miss Sophia. If she was in love and her family opposed the match, then things were going to go badly for her and it would not help matters for everyone to know that she'd slipped off, unchaperoned, to meet a young man in the woods. And there was more!

When I next saw Will he gave me the news that he had ferried across the same naval gentleman again and, though he had cheerily asked him where he was bound and whether he was new to the area, the young man had not given any proper reply but seemed, Will said, very anxious.

Lovelorn was the word, I thought to myself.

The weather grew warmer and my dairy became the nicest, coolest place to be. Sometimes I even scoured things that didn't really need scouring, or slowly reordered my tins and containers along their shelves, rather than have Mrs Bonny find me something else to do in the cloying heat of the kitchens.

One evening, finishing supper early, I walked down to the river to collect Betsy and, it being so muggy and unpleasant, Will proposed that we should dip in the water to try and cool ourselves.

'In fact,' he said, 'I will teach both my girls to swim.'

Betsy squealed with delight, while I protested that we could not possibly do such a thing, that the waterweeds would wrap themselves around our legs, drag us down and drown us.

Will laughed. 'The weeds haven't caught me yet!' he said, for he swam across the river and back again every morning. I would not be persuaded, however, and watched fearfully as Betsy stripped down until she was as naked as a duck and plunged in, shrieking. Another thing that stopped me from going in was that I could not dream of being naked before Will, yet how could I swim in my stays, smock and petticoats?

Will had no such modesty and, stripped to his breeches in the water, was uncommon patient with Betsy, holding her up, turning her over so that she learned to float on her back and teaching her to scrabble in the water like a dog. She found such amusement in it that she didn't want to come out, and as a consequence was so tired when she did emerge that she fell asleep almost straight away. Will had to walk us both back to the hall, carrying Betsy over his shoulder.

Going indoors, the others told me that there had been more raised voices in the drawing room that evening and that, unbeknown to Mrs Bonny or Mr Griffin,

Patience had gone up with a handful of scouring sand which she'd 'accidentally' dropped on the hall floor, near the drawing-room door. She had then, very slowly, brushed it up, listening all the while. That night in our bedroom she told Prudence and me that she had heard Lady Cecilia say that unless Miss Sophia ceased all communication with 'a certain person' then she would be cast out of the family forthwith and have to make her own way in the world.

The following day I became involved in the dispute myself.

It was a very warm evening and I decided to walk down to the river to collect Betsy again and, if I could not bring myself to swim, at least dip my toes in the water to cool off. My cows were happily chewing the cud in the second field and I called a greeting to them as I passed, only to feel mighty silly when I realised that someone had overheard me.

'Good evening!' a voice called in response, and I looked across to see a young gentleman in naval officer's uniform standing behind a tree. He had not come over on the ferry, that was clear, for his horse was grazing nearby.

Automatically, I curtseyed.

'You are the dairymaid at Bridgeford Hall, are you not?'

'I am, sir,' I said, knowing immediately that this must be *he*, Miss Sophia's young gentleman.

This was confirmed by his next words. 'I have heard

both the Misses speak of you. I believe you kindly supplied the cow for the *tableau vivant?*'

'I did, sir.' I indicated the cows in the field. 'That was Daisy, that was.' He began fumbling in his jacket pocket for something, and to fill the silence I found myself rambling on, giving him the names of the other cows and telling him that Clover was new and frisky, which I am sure he didn't find the least bit interesting.

At last he pulled something out of his jacket and said, 'I was hoping I might see someone from the house. I wonder if I can trust your discretion?'

I nodded, thrilled. 'Indeed you can, sir. Do you want me to take a message to . . . to someone in the hall?'

'To Miss Sophia, yes,' he said, and he pressed a folded, sealed paper into my hand. 'Let no one else see it – not even her sister!'

'Of course not, sir,' I said. I pointed to the river. 'There is a child I have to collect from the ferryman but I'll give the note to Miss Sophia on my return.'

'I hoped to see her myself but I have to return to my ship forthwith.'

'You can trust me, sir,' I said.

He bowed slightly (which endeared him to me, for it is not something which gentry often do to maidservants), mounted his horse and rode off, leaving me staring after him and marvelling.

I looked at the letter, which was addressed in a flowing, educated hand, and blessed the day that I had been taught my letters, for I could read that it said: *The Honourable Miss Sophia Baysmith* and *By hand*. I put it carefully into the pocket of my petticoat and carried on walking down to the river.

There was a little bit of a panic when I got there, for Betsy had vanished while Will was on the other side of the river with a passenger. Eventually, after much running hither and thither, we found her flat on her back fast asleep by a rabbit hole, where she'd been sitting waiting for a rabbit to emerge. By this time, because of the anxious ten minutes or so spent looking for Betsy, I'd forgotten about the note in my pocket.

Leaving her asleep, Will and I spoke at our relief in finding her – Will saying that at least he'd taught her to keep her head above water, so while he'd been searching he'd been confident she hadn't drowned.

'You must learn to swim, too,' he said.

The thought of dipping my body into smooth, cool water was so enticing just then that before I knew it I had taken off my outer smock, bodice and skirt and was standing (still covered, mind, a lot better than some Society young ladies) in my stays and petticoats.

Will, sensing my embarrassment, endeavoured to be very matter of fact and, acting just as if I were fully dressed, backed into the river holding both his arms out straight in front of him. He told me to follow him in whilst holding tightly on to his hands and kicking up my legs. I did this and so enjoyed the feeling of lightness and well-being that I found myself jumping backwards and forwards, first going on my back and then on my front, my petticoats floating about me in the water.

'You can do it if you're confident,' he said. 'A few more lessons and you'll be swimming as well as me. Now, why don't you sit on the bank in the sun a little while and dry yourself as best you can.'

I went to sit near Betsy, who was still asleep, and it wasn't until I began to pat myself dry with a rough cloth of Will's that I remembered: the letter. I had been in the water with the letter still in my pocket!

Will hauled himself out of the water and came to sit beside me, then took one look at my stricken face and asked me what was wrong.

'Miss Sophia's young man!' I said. 'I met him and he gave me a note for her . . .'

Very gingerly, I felt in my petticoat pocket and pulled it out, soaking wet. I handled it very carefully, but it fell into four pieces, each a blotchy mess of blue ink and totally indecipherable. The only thing still in one piece was the young gentleman's seal, which had a dolphin on it.

Horrified, I began weeping – waking Betsy, who cried in empathy with me.

'He told me to take it to her . . . He said to tell no one!' I said. 'And now look at it!'

Will sat Betsy on his lap and comforted the both of us as best he could, and after some discussion we decided that I should go straight to Miss Sophia and confess what had happened. Thus I went into Will's hut, took off my wet petticoats and put on my gown, then walked with

Betsy back to the barn where one of her 'sisters' put her to bed for the night.

In the kitchens I found a great debate under way as to whether young ladies should be forced to marry men of their father's choice or be able to follow their hearts. Another time I would have joined in and spoken up strongly on the side of love, but that evening I was too anxious about Miss Sophia's letter to think of anything else. How was I going to approach Miss Sophia? What excuse could I use and what would the rest of her family think? Surreptitiously passing her a note was one thing, but actually approaching, speaking, explaining and apologising to her was another.

I beckoned to Patience to leave the servants' discussion for a moment. 'Do you know where Miss Sophia is?' I asked her, for the family's supper hour was long past and the two young ladies could be anywhere.

'Miss Sophia?' she replied cheerily. 'Halfway to Bath by now, I should think.'

I didn't understand and thought she was making a joke. 'What do you mean? How so?'

'It's what we've all been talking of,' she said. 'Weren't you listening?'

'I heard all the talk about whether or not one should obey one's father but I've been out of the house for near two hours. Has something happened here?' I asked urgently.

'Why, yes: Miss Sophia has been sent away in the carriage to stay with her uncle.'

'Never!'

' 'Tis true. And 'tis because of a young man she's been meeting in secret. Milord was heard to say that he was a naval man and, being without a title or a fortune, quite unsuitable. He called him a varlet and a fortune hunter!'

I stared at her, shocked.

'She's never to see him again!' said Patience, enthralled in the telling. 'There must be as many miles as possible between the two of them.'

I stared at Patience. '*Really?* She's been sent to Bath?'

'She left an hour ago, crying her eyes out. She's been allowed to take Christina with her, but must not return until the new year,' said Patience.

I sat down at the table, tears filling my eyes. Now she would never know that her sweetheart had sent her a letter. And he would never know that she had not received it.

It seemed that love was not always an excellent thing.

Chapter Seven

The house was very quiet in the days following Miss Sophia's departure, and it was apparent that Miss Alice missed her dreadfully, for she was to be seen moping about the place with red eyes. There was some talk of her being sent to be with her sister, but in the end she stayed – and on warm days sat in the park under the big oak where her parents had been painted, sometimes with her maid, sometimes alone, but always with a book in her hands. Lady Cecilia arranged a variety of amusements for her: a picnic, various musical events and a visiting landscape painter, but anyone could see that Miss Alice was pining for her sister. At one time I thought of telling her about the note and confessing what had happened to it, but I was worried that this was not the correct thing to do, for hadn't the young man said that no one must know, not even Miss Alice? Besides, what difference could it make to anything now that Miss Sophia had been sent away? Finally, I decided: I knew I would have the opportunity to speak to Miss Sophia when she returned after Christmas, so I resolved to try and forget about it until then.

One humid evening Betsy and I had another swimming lesson with Will. Betsy, trusting fully in her brother, managed to scramble quite a distance in the water, but I, not quite so sure of being able to stay afloat, thought it a great achievement when I managed to take my feet off the riverbed and float on my back for a few moments without being held.

Afterwards, as we sat drying off, Will told me that he had had news of his relations in London. A cousin from Kent had gone to join them and sent a message back to say that the family was having a new boat built, one that could hold twelve passengers. This meant that, when full, each trip across the Thames would earn them the sum of four shillings.

'And four shillings back again!' Will told me, marvelling at it. 'Although there would need to be two strong watermen in the boat, of course, to row across that many passengers.'

'And you think you are that strong waterman, do you?' I teased.

'Indeed. My cousin said they are waiting for me.'

We were silent for a moment.

'But what of Betsy?' I said, for I still didn't want to go to London and she was an excellent reason not to. 'Even if I could find work there –'

'You can and would!' Will interrupted. 'There are thousands of well-to-do folk in London, needing thousands of servants to look after them.'

'Even if I could find work, what would we do with Betsy in London?' I repeated. 'She couldn't just be left to fend for herself all day.'

Will heaved a sigh. 'I know. 'Tis a problem.'

'And you would surely not go without us.'

'My two girls?' Will said. 'As if I could . . .'

'Is it so bad here?'

'Not . . . *bad*. It's just that we will never make anything of ourselves.'

'There are compensations,' I said, and I made a gesture with my arms, taking in the beautiful grounds, the orchard and the sunset reflected on the river, then leaned over and kissed him. He forgot about London then, and – kissing and being kissed – so did I, until Betsy came back crying that a dormouse had bitten her.

In mid-August, there were various parties held at the house and visitors from London coming and going, and Miss Alice was allowed to Bath to see her sister. We learned afterwards, in whispered snippets of news, that Miss Sophia desperately wanted to come home, but this was still not going to be allowed until after Christmas. By that time, so Lord Baysmith had apparently discovered, her young naval officer would be on his way to Australia and well out of harm's way. Patience, after some listening at doors and skulking around corners, assured us that Lord Baysmith had now selected the man who would be Miss Sophia's future husband and she was to be introduced to him soon. Following this, there was a lot of speculation amongst us as to who this gentleman might be and whether he would be titled, worth a fortune, or perhaps have both these desirable qualities. I joined in, but ached inside for Miss Sophia.

Two more things happened in August, the first being that Mrs Bonny taught me how to make soft cheeses, which I was very pleased about, for it was another skill that – if I ever had to find a new job – would stand me in good stead. The other thing which happened in August, however, was not at all good. It was, in fact, devastating.

It was the last day of the month and Betsy had set off to spend it at the river as usual. It was a slightly misty morning, for the season was just on the verge of turning autumnal, and I was thinking to myself that when the days grew shorter either Will or I would have to bring Betsy backwards and forwards, for unless there was a moon it would be pitch-dark, and even with a candle she couldn't be expected to go across the fields on her own. She waved to me when she reached the river and, though I did not see Will waving back, I presumed he was there and just ferrying someone across.

An hour or so went by and I had finished with my cows, wiped them down, put them back to pasture and was about to begin the lengthy process of churning butter when I heard Betsy running back towards the dairy, sobbing heartily with every step she took.

I stopped turning the handle of the churn and ran outside thinking she had hurt herself in some way, but her face was so pale, so shocked, that I knew it was something much worse than this.

'Will's not there!' she cried. 'He's gone!'

I picked her up and hugged her. 'What do you mean? I expect he's over on the other side of the river.'

'No! He's not. I waited and waited and looked everywhere, but he's gone away!'

My first thought was that he had drowned and, terrified and anxious that Betsy should not know this, I put her in the care of one of her 'sisters' and said that I would go down and sort things out, that he was sure to be there and perhaps he was just having a game of hide-and-seek. Not even waiting to find Mrs Bonny and tell her where I was going, I ran down the field as fast as I could, twice tripping over my feet in my anxiety. As I ran I looked for his boat, hoping to see it plying its way back from the other side of the river, but when I got a little nearer I realised that it was pulled right up on the opposite bank, just as if Will had taken a fare over and stayed on that side. I also saw that there were two men and a woman standing on the landing stage on *this* side: passengers waiting to be taken across.

When I reached them, I could hardly breathe enough to speak. 'Is he not here?' I asked desperately, and the three of them shook their heads.

'I have been waiting near half an hour!' said the first in line, the baker's boy. 'I've a full tray of bread for the

Millbridge market. I've never known him be away so long before.'

'Nor I,' said the woman. 'Where can he be?'

I ran into his hut and, though admittedly it was difficult to tell, it didn't look as if his canvas bed and rough old blanket had been slept in. I looked under the bed, where he'd kept a tin box containing a few things that had belonged to his parents, but this box had gone – as had his oilskin cape, his boots, spare shirts and extra pair of breeches. I went outside again, crying with shock, and informed the others.

'Perhaps a thief in the night . . .' the woman said, but I shook my head wordlessly. I already had my suspicions about where he'd gone.

'He liked a swim in the mornings,' the second man said, and then offered to swim across to the Millbridge side of the river, just to 'make sure he's not over there'. This was what he said, but what he meant was that he wanted to make sure Will was not in the water somewhere, caught up in weeds, drowned in the deep water. He stripped to his breeches and dived in, while the rest of us poked about in the shallows and amongst the bulrushes, but they knew, of course – and I knew – that if his possessions had gone, then he must have gone with them. And I could guess where.

'He was always talking about London,' said the baker's boy, when the other man had swum across and reported that he had seen nothing untoward. He looked at me sympathetically. 'Shall I go over, get the ferry boat and row it back?'

I shook my head and told him to leave it on the other side, saying that if Will had gone off for the day somewhere, on his return he would want to find the boat exactly where he'd left it.

'In the meantime, what shall we do for a ferryman?' said the woman, tutting impatiently. 'My daughter lives in Millbridge and is expecting me to look after her children. She can't go to work otherwise. I must get over!'

We discussed this – or they did, while I stared across the water, shocked and speechless. The baker's boy said he knew someone else with a boat and he would ask this man to run a temporary service 'until Will comes back'.

'If he ever does,' I said.

I sat there with Betsy on my lap until the next milking time, both of us watching the river flowing on and on towards the sea and feeling totally desolate. I knew that I would never see him again, for if he had truly loved me, surely he would have stayed by my side.

Chapter Eight

'Have you heard from your sweetheart yet?' Patience asked a few weeks later.

I pretended not to hear her, which was foolish because it meant she had to say it again, but louder, so it seemed to me that everyone in the kitchens heard and there was a moment when everything stopped; the servants ceased pounding, kneading, polishing, scouring or crimping and waited to hear what I was going to say in reply.

I felt my face flush. 'No, I haven't. Not yet,' I said stiffly.

Of course I hadn't. I didn't think, in all the time I'd been working at the hall, that any of the kitchen staff had ever received a letter. If they had, it would have been a minor sensation and Patience and everyone else would most certainly have heard of it. Letters sometimes came for Milord and Lady, and for the aristocracy and Honourables and plain wealthy ladies and gentlemen who stayed at the hall, but never for any of us.

'But I don't suppose your lad is clever with ink and parchment, is he?' she persisted.

I shrugged.

'Though even if he can't write, he could surely have got a message to you by some other means.' On this, too, being received by me in silence, she added, 'The cheek of the devil, some lads! Fancy him up and leaving you with his little sister to care for.'

I think she would have gone on provoking me until I snapped back, but thankfully Mrs Bonny appeared from the still room. 'That's enough chatter from both of you,' she said. 'Go back and make sure the butter has come together, Kitty. We need it for supper.'

I nodded and escaped, taking my irritation out on the butter churner and turning the handle so hard and fast that the whey came off, the butter came together and then began to separate again so that I only just caught it in time.

I had been desperately miserable in the days that followed Will's departure. At first I couldn't believe he had really gone; for a day or more I thought that he must be playing some sort of trick on us and would appear, laughing and teasing us for being worried. After that I almost convinced myself that he must have rowed over to Millbridge to buy something and had had an accident, but the fact that all his possessions had disappeared didn't make sense of this explanation. And why hadn't he left me a note? He might not have been able to write a whole, proper letter – in fact, I knew he wouldn't have been able to do that – but he could at least have scribed a few words: *I will send for you soon* or *I love you* or even just *Sorry*, and added his name. I found nothing, however, even though I practically took the hut to pieces. Why hadn't he left us anything? The obvious answer was that he was too embarrassed about leaving us; too ashamed of himself.

After I'd wept enough to fill a milking bucket, I began to grow angry. How dare he just go off and leave Betsy with me? How despicable! I became so resentful of him then, so furious, that for a time I almost wished he'd drowned in the river rather than stopped loving me. For I knew he must have stopped loving me to go away.

The day we found out he'd disappeared I'd finally quelled my own tears, then sat Betsy down quietly and told her that Will had gone to London to make his fortune and one day would come back again, a rich man, and take us to live in a big house. She didn't believe me – but then I didn't believe me, either – and for two whole weeks she stopped speaking. I observed her with her little friends, saw her standing watching their games, occasionally nodding or shaking her head in response to a direct question. She barely ate, and became pale and sad, while I seethed with rage about Will, furious at what he'd done, and longed for some means to inform him just what misery his selfish actions had caused.

Mrs Bonny was very kind to both of us. Betsy, of course, no longer took her meals with Will, so on the face of it was costing the household money, but for those first two weeks she hardly ate a thing anyway, just kept going on some ends of cheese which she nibbled like a mouse. After two weeks or so her appetite and speech began, gradually, to return, but she still didn't cost a lot to keep, for she would either share my portion or help herself to a ladleful of meat and vegetables from the stewpot which hung permanently over the fire. It was a rich household and there was no need for anyone ever to go hungry.

More pressing was the question of where Betsy would go during the day in the winter, for the other children either had little jobs on the farm or went back to spend the day with their mothers. A very young child in a dairy, however, is a danger to itself and others. For the first few days, she wanted nothing more than to go down to Will's hut and, after looking in it carefully to make sure that he hadn't arrived back in the night, stare endlessly over to the other side of the river, where the ferry boat still stood, saying, 'But where has he gone?' and looking far more miserable than any five-year-old should ever do.

Wanting to keep her occupied and entertained, I hit upon the idea of encouraging her to learn how to make the simplest of corn dollies from lengths of straw. These proved popular, and she gradually made them for all the children and then moved on to the adults. Pressing these on the other servants, she would wish them a good day and give them a solemn smile, and as a consequence became quite a favourite – everyone had a greeting or a sweetmeat for the poor little orphan girl who'd been abandoned first by her sister then by her brother.

As for me, I feared that they just thought me a fool to have been taken in by him.

September wore on and the whole family went to Bath to take the waters. They met Miss Sophia there, who, according to more scraps of news which fluttered down to us from Faith, begged to be allowed home, but was refused. To retaliate, and still pining for her lost love, she was rude to the man whom her father had particularly wanted her to meet. By way of contrast, Miss Alice had attended the Assembly Rooms every night and danced on several occasions with a man who was a literary figure as well as being, word had it, worth ten thousand a year. She was, apparently, quite besotted with him, and Lord and Lady Baysmith were said to be pleased with the match.

Later in September, Miss Alice had two lady cousins staying with her, so the house seemed a merrier place. Betsy, very much admiring their gowns and their hair ornaments, took to watching their various comings and goings from the house and had soon made them all corn dollies, which she was too shy to present to them but which I passed on by means of their maids. Subsequently, these Misses – bored and, I think, seeking to do Good Works – asked to meet Betsy. They came to the dairy one afternoon and Mrs Bonny had me dress Betsy in a clean smock and present her as a poor little abandoned child – which, I suppose, was exactly what she was. Betsy curtseyed very prettily and the young ladies each gave her a silver coin. Though it was but an amusement for them, it made Betsy smile again.

By the end of September everyone in the house owned at least one corn dolly, and Mrs Bonny professed to be anxious about them, saying that – seeing as they were fertility symbols – she hoped she wasn't going to lose all her girls to motherhood.

At the beginning of October the weather suddenly turned and I started to worry not only about what Betsy was going to do in the winter, but what she was going to wear, for she had no warm clothes, no outer garments or strong boots to wear when the rain was lashing down or it was snowing. I grew angry with Will again. Why hadn't he thought of that? Why hadn't he sent money from London or made some provision for Betsy before he went? She badly needed a set of winter clothes and, even more – the poor lamb – a kindly mother and father to nurture her, but clothes and foster families cost money and I had none. In all this time I had not heard a word from Betsy's sister Kate, either, and wondered, if she ever came back, whether she would even know where to find the child.

The cousins departed and Miss Alice returned to her books, now reading them in the drawing room in front of the fire or sometimes, if her mother was not at home, in the *petit salon*. One afternoon, with Faith on an errand somewhere and the other staff busy, I was asked to take in more clotted cream for Miss Alice's afternoon scones, so I quickly found a clean smock for myself, scooped some cream into a dish and carried it up on a tray.

She barely registered my presence at first, so engrossed was she in the book she was reading, but just pointed to the table and motioned for me to put the dish down. Suddenly, however – for she was not usually so ungracious – she seemed to realise what she was doing and spoke up quickly to thank me.

'I fear my mind was elsewhere, Kitty,' she added. 'I have been thinking of nothing else but the book I'm reading.'

I knew precious little about books, so merely waited to see if she was going to say anything else.

'Sometimes, if I am engrossed in a book, I even forget to eat,' she went on in a confiding and friendly manner. 'The other night I read by candlelight until three in the morning!'

'It must be a very good book to make you do that, miss,' I said.

'It is, and – what do you think? It is by a *lady*.'

She sounded surprised by this and I pulled a surprised face, too, although I had no way of knowing whether this was unusual, good, bad or indifferent.

'A new friend, a literary gentleman, told me about her, and I am most anxious to obtain her newest novel, but it has completely sold out. I've even tried to get hold of one second-hand, but no one wants to part with such a precious book. It is quite the most fashionable thing to be seen reading at the moment.'

'Really, miss?' Ah, I thought, the literary gentleman must be the new suitor I'd heard about.

'They are reprinting it next month and I've begged my father to go to the publisher's in London to secure a copy, but he's told me he will be out of the country at that time.' She sighed. 'I'd ask for one to be sent in the mail, but I fear such valuable volumes would be stolen.'

'Couldn't you go to London yourself, miss?' I asked.

'Oh heavens, no. The roads are shocking at the moment and jolt one to pieces.' She frowned. 'I could send Faith but then she suffers dreadfully with travel-sickness.' She sat up and spread a scone liberally with jam, then cream. 'I fear that the book will sell out again immediately, for it is terribly *à la mode.*'

'Yes, miss.'

'Every stylish person will be speaking about it and I shall have nothing to say!'

This did not seem such an awful dilemma, not compared to my own, but I tried to smile sympatheti-cally before bobbing a curtsey and turning towards the door.

Before I'd reached it, however, Miss Alice said, 'Kitty, wait! I've just had a rather marvellous idea.'

I turned back.

'Perhaps you could go to London for me!'

I stopped, my hand on the door handle. '*Me*, miss?'

'Yes, why not? You could go to the publisher's in

Whitehall, and stay a day or so in a discreet guest house. It would be a great adventure for you. What do you think?'

London! I thought. And then I thought of Will and what I would say to him as I handed over Betsy.

'Yes, miss,' I said. 'I'd be happy to do that.'

Chapter Nine

'**Y**ou're never!' Patience said, gawping at me. '*London?*'

'Yes, London,' I said, as if I went there and back every day.

'But where will you stay? And what have you got to do when you get there?'

'I'm going to stay in a boarding house,' I said. 'Miss is arranging it herself. And all I have to do is go to a publisher's office and buy a book for her.'

'What book? The Bible or something?'

'No, it's a story published in three volumes,' I said, Miss Alice having filled me in on the details. 'It's called *Pride and Prejudice* and it's written by a lady. It's completely sold out.' I paused, then added, 'Every fashionable person is reading it.'

'But what did Mrs Bonny have to say about you going? Didn't she mind?'

'She couldn't say much,' I said, 'because it was Lady

Cecilia who told her about it.'

Mrs Bonny had, in fact, been very good once she had known that Betsy wasn't going to be left behind with her. She had suggested ways we could make ourselves more comfortable on the journey, told me what to do to prevent travel-sickness and promised to prepare a sleeping draught for me. The stagecoach to London would take near twenty-eight hours, with short stops to change the horses and take refreshment, and one overnight stop at an inn. The coach would take us to Charing Cross (the very centre of London, so Miss Alice had informed me) and a letter had been sent ahead to a respectable guest house to secure a room. When I got there, I intended that Betsy and I should sleep for a few hours, then walk to St Paul's to find the cousins, wait for Will to appear and confront him with Betsy.

I spent a considerable amount of time imagining this confrontation, thinking of how shocked he would look to see us, of what I would say and how he would reply. I would remain calm, icy with disdain. I'd cry, *'How dare you treat us so!'*, *'You have used me ill!'* and other noble and haughty utterances.

The trouble was, I just couldn't imagine myself saying those things, being contemptuous and all. I knew Betsy would probably fling herself into his arms and was concerned that I, being so thankful to see him again, might do that, too. What if I broke down and made a pathetic fool of myself, begged him to come back and said that I would forgive him everything? I sighed heartily when I considered this and tried to stiffen my resolve.

It had been agreed that in my absence, Patience was going to work in the dairy. She would do all the basic tasks, the scouring and boiling of the pans and equipment, and would make butter and cream under Mrs Bonny's supervision, but the actual milking of the cows would be done by one of the cow-keepers who worked at the big farm. Discovering this, I felt rather anxious about my dear animals having just anyone, maybe a different person every day, come and milk them, for I was used to them and their little ways and they were used to me. I knew that Buttercup liked to be sung to as she was milked, that Clover (the new Clover) was apt to kick out with her left foot, that Daisy did not like the sun and that Rose, who grew irritable and fidgety if kept waiting, should be milked before the others. I wondered how my cows would like waiting for the big herd of black-and-whites to be milked before they got their turn, and if they would give as much milk without me being there to coax it out of them. I was perfectly sure they would not.

I was due to leave for London two weeks after my conversation with Miss Alice, and during that time Patience spent most days by my side learning my duties: how to set the milk in cream pans, heat it and then skim off the thick crust of clotted cream which formed; how to work the fresh butter on a board and decorate the breakfast rounds of it with Milord's insignia. While we worked, she obliged me with her opinions on London and all the perils I'd face on the journey there.

'Highwaymen are rife on the turnpike roads,' she said. 'They stop you practically every mile of the way. I've heard a story about someone whose carriage was held up three times. The first thief took his pocket watch, the second his money and the next his clothes. He arrived in London as naked as the day he was born.'

'Ah well, I'll take my chances,' I said. 'I don't think a highwayman would be interested in wearing my petticoats.'

'And don't trust the maidservants at any inn you stop at along the way! I know an old lady who had a sleeping draught put in her hot milk at night and woke to find her wigs and all her hats had been taken. She had to continue her journey completely bald.'

Will was another favourite topic of hers. 'Suppose you can't find him? Suppose he turns his back on you? Suppose he has another sweetheart now – a London girl? London girls are terrible forward, they say. He might not have been able to resist.'

'It's nothing to me if he has or hasn't resisted,' I lied. 'I'm not going there to see him, but to get the book for Miss and then restore Betsy to her rightful family.'

'I bet he had it planned all along,' Patience said. 'I daresay it was in his mind when he first started walking out with you. I fear you've been awful gullible.'

I fumed but said nothing, and on my bad days thought she was probably right.

*

I'd told Betsy where we were going, of course; explained that we were going to find Will so she could live with him again. I added that I would miss her very much, but said when she was a big girl she could come back and visit me whenever she liked. She seemed pleased about this and began to talk about what she would do in London, but then just before we left she found out that there was going to be a bonfire and fireworks on November the fifth and we were going to miss it.

'The other children have been talking about it all day,' she said. 'It's going to be the biggest bonfire in the world.' She looked at me miserably. 'And they're going to have sugar cakes to eat.'

'We can get sugar cakes in London,' I said, 'and ice cream and gingerbread and marchpane, too.'

'We can't get rides on the hay wagon.'

'No, not those, but we're going to travel to London on a big, big stagecoach and when we're there you'll see shops – oh, no end of shops – and carriages and sedan chairs and fine ladies and maybe even the King, with a golden crown!' I was making up this last bit, for the King was mad again and was not to be seen anywhere, with or without his crown.

'But there won't be dancing in London.'

'That's where you're wrong,' I said. 'There's always dancing in London.' I remembered what the Misses had told me. 'The milkmaids twirl down the road garlanded with flowers!' I assured her. I had a sudden rush of inspiration. 'And you must take Will and his family some corn dollies! They don't have such things in London and they'll be vastly pleased with them.'

This last did the trick and she spent that day and the next few plaiting, weaving and tying in straws with her grubby little fingers for all she was worth.

We were travelling on the top of the coach, for the inside seats were much more expensive. Besides, Miss Alice explained, only the gentry rode within and they would not take kindly at having to share their space with a servant. Because we were outside, Miss Alice had loaned me a thick fur rug to wrap about us and also a strong travelling bag made of leather called a portmanteau. This was so heavy and cumbersome that I tried to leave it behind and take my perfectly good cloth bag, but Miss Alice pointed out that it wasn't merely for our spare clothes but to keep her precious new book safe and dry during the journey home.

'Stow the money securely inside, and be sure to keep the address of the lodging house and the publisher's safe there, too,' she said the evening before we were to leave. 'You must go there before you do anything else. And where are you to find him?' she asked, testing me.

'Whitehall,' I responded. 'A road off Trafalgar Square.'

'Quite right. And insist that you must have the book after travelling so far, no matter how many advance orders they have for it. It's in three volumes – I told you that, didn't I?'

'You did, miss.'

'You may use my name, and Father's name, in order to secure it.'

'If you say so, Miss Alice,' I said, rather nervous at this thought.

'Once you have the volumes,' she went on, 'then you may go and do a little sightseeing.' She began counting coins into a small drawstring bag. 'The three volumes cost eighteen shillings,' she said, 'and here are another twenty shillings for your lodgings and food.'

I thanked her, a little overwhelmed, for I had never seen so much money before.

'Guard it well,' she continued, 'and don't be led astray by London ways and London tricks. Remember there are card sharps on every corner and quacks selling miracles on every street.'

'Yes, miss, I'll remember,' I said.

'I am sure you won't do anything silly, for Mrs Bonny has told me that you are sensible and resourceful. Now, I shall be simply desperate for my book, but the journey is arduous and you will need to rest after, so I won't expect to see you for a week or so.'

I bobbed a curtsey and went out, my pocket heavy but my heart light. I was about to have an adventure.

In spite of all that I had heard against it, I was very excited to be going to London. I would have been even more excited if I'd been setting out on Will's invitation and not because of his abandonment of us, but to be going at all was thrill enough, for this was something that few people in Bridgeford had ever done.

At six o'clock the next morning, Betsy and I bade goodbye to the other servants (I also said farewell to my dear cows) and rode on one of the carts out of the farmyard, heading for the Stag and Hounds in Thorndyke, where we were to catch the stagecoach. As we left I looked down towards Will's hut – just in case – but, of course, he wasn't there, only his boat still pulled on to the opposite bank. Of the man who had taken over his ferry service there was no sign, and I had already heard that he was most unreliable compared to Will.

Thinking of that, I felt a little bitter, for I had always assumed that Will was completely trustworthy, both to ferry a person across the river or to fall in love with. I vowed that when I found him I would tell him that he couldn't just play around with people, pick them up and put them down as he saw fit, and that saying you loved someone wasn't something that should be done lightly.

Seeing the stagecoach waiting, with its six horses stamping their feet in eagerness to be off, thrilled us both, and I was mighty thankful that Betsy was a strong and resilient little girl, for some children of barely five years would have screamed to high heaven at being handed up to the top of a carriage and having to sit on a wavering, jolting seat, buffeted about by the wind and swaying this way and that. I climbed aloft after Betsy, and oh, how precarious it was up there, how shallow the seats, how vulnerable I felt! Gingerly, I made my way to the back and discovered that there were eight seats on the top, including those of the driver and groom. I put Miss Alice's leather bag on the floor under my legs, tucked her fur rug around us and prepared myself, rather nervous now, for the journey.

A large, plump man hauled himself up next and took the place beside me, and I lifted Betsy on to my lap to allow him a little more room. Two older men joined, and then a youth who, judging by the pile of books that he carried in a leather strap, was a student going back to school. There was one last man, wearing a dark suit with a clergyman's collar, and when he was in his seat and a heap of luggage had been piled upon the roof in the middle, the three inside passengers came from within the tavern and climbed aboard. From what I could see from my insecure perch, they appeared to be three women of similar colouring but of different generations, perhaps grandmother, mother and daughter. They were in mourning and I thought to myself that, chances were, the grandfather of the family had died in London and they were going to his funeral but, of course, I never found out.

The coach set off and Betsy screamed and so did I, for with the first jolt it seemed that we would be dashed to the floor of the coach or, worse, thrown out into the road. I held on to the nearest thing, which happened to be the stout man, and he acted like some sort of ballast and did not seem to mind my clutching him. Betsy and I soon realised, however, that passengers must move in rhythm with the galloping of the horses and the swaying of the coach, and once we had this under control I apologised to the man and moved a little distance away – for I had discerned by then that, far from being offended that I was holding him, he was only too eager to put a steadying arm around my waist.

At first it was a novelty to ride atop a carriage, to see over fences and splash in and out of puddles, to sway around corners and have people stare and wave as we thundered through villages, but about half an hour after we set off, the novelty had quite palled as we were jolted, windswept and terrified by turns. Betsy was saved quite a bit of the bumping as she was sitting on my lap, but even though I pulled a fold of the fur rug underneath me, my rear ached dreadfully and I would have sold one of my own cows for a cushion. I even thought it would be a welcome relief to be stopped by a highwayman, for at least that would mean a little rest from the incessant jolting.

Some many miles later, our faces frozen, we stopped at a coaching inn to change the horses, and the landlord came out to urge us to come inside, saying there was a side of beef roasting on the spit. I was very tempted by this but, though I had plenty of money safely stowed in the portmanteau, had been warned several times that London was a most expensive city, and so declined. Betsy and I made sure to use the inn's privy, however, then sat on a settle in a passageway and, while sniffing at the roasting meat, ate the bread and cheese which Mrs Bonny had provided. All too soon the ostler rang a handbell to round everyone up and we were ushered aboard the stagecoach and off it went again.

And so proceeded the day, pausing at various coaching inns to change the steaming, panting horses, until at nine o'clock we stopped for the night and I felt I could have cried with thankfulness. I didn't think it had been too bad a journey for Betsy, for my body had cushioned her and the galloping of the horses acted like a rocking cradle to send her off to sleep, but I had felt every jolt, every bump, every pothole in the road, and had a constant fear that I would be thrown off and end up dead in a ditch. The only thing which redeemed this sad prospect was imagining Will finding out, realising that I had died in the act of looking for him and feeling guilty about it for the rest of his life.

As I climbed down with shaking legs, all too enthusiastically assisted by the stout man, I thanked God that Miss Alice had opted for us to stay in an inn overnight, for some of the fastest stagecoaches travelled right through the day and night and I could not have borne this. Though our room in the Dove and Partridge was shabby, the mattress was soft and I fell asleep straight away, not stirring until a maid knocked on the door at six o'clock the next morning with a jug of washing water.

The only section of the journey I could have said I almost enjoyed was the last, when we entered London and I began seeing lovely buildings, churches, lavish gardens, green spaces and beautiful houses. I'd been told that London was a dark and treacherous place, but I saw that in some parts it was not; that in some parts there were gardens and fine dwellings enough to make a person gasp.

'Have you and your little daughter got a place to stay?' the stout man asked me as the river came into view.

'My daughter!' I exclaimed. 'She is my sw–' But no, I was not about to tell him my life story. 'She is my sister,' I amended.

'Oh, of course,' he said. Then he bent over and said in my ear, 'Your secret is safe with me, my dear.'

My cheeks flamed. What did he take me for?

'Got lodgings, have you?' he asked again.

'Yes, we have somewhere to stay, I thank you,' I said in a very clipped manner. And I couldn't resist adding, 'And besides, I am only in London to visit a publisher for my mistress.' With luck, he would think me a lady's maid and too high for his advances.

His reply, if there had been one, was drowned out by us suddenly wheeling around the corner, coming upon Charing Cross and being startled by a cacophony of sounds: shouts, bells, iron wheels turning on stone, whips cracking and peddlers calling their wares. Staring around us in astonishment, Betsy and I saw stagecoaches, carriages, hackney cabs, sedan chairs and people on horseback, all crowded higgledy-piggledy on the cobbles. Surely, I thought, all the population of the city was gathered here together, for I had never seen so many people before in all my life.

How small I felt then, and nervous, and wished so much that Will was there to meet us and claim us. I reminded myself, however, that I was a resourceful girl – that's what Miss Alice had called me, anyway – and that we'd reached London safely and not lost anything.

'In what direction is St Paul's?' I asked the stout man while the driver was negotiating our coach into position.

'Why, it's straight across there!' he said, pointing down a busy street I later found out was the Strand. 'You can just see the dome.'

I looked where he was pointing and, from our vantage point on top of the coach, saw it rising above every other building, something gold sparkling on its pinnacle. So close! Oh, I was surely very near to finding Will!

I looked around me, marvelling. 'Such a lot of people!' I blurted out.

'Doctor Johnson said that one finds the full tide of human existence at Charing Cross,' my stout travelling companion pronounced, and I nodded politely, although I did not know who Dr Johnson was.

There were dandies, too, whom I had only heard about before: one man, immaculate in purple velvet, white shirt and starched cravat, was sniffing delicately at the bunch of herbs he carried, while another man was talking to him, hand on hip, in an affected pose. Betsy especially stared at him, for he was wearing a gold lace suit with a purple tricorne hat trimmed with feathers.

'Allow me to lift you down,' said the stout man when the carriage had stopped fully.

'No, that is quite –' I began, but it was too late; he had seized me around the waist and lifted me over the guard rail and out on to the cobbles. Betsy followed likewise and the fur rug fell to the ground around us.

'If you wouldn't mind reaching for my portmanteau,' I said, and he did so, placing it at my feet, where I covered it with the fur rug. He gave me a funny little bow, bending only as far as a very stout man can, but did not move on.

'Do you wish me to call you a hackney cab?' he asked, but a smartly dressed woman tapped him on the shoulder with her fan and, with a movement of her head, indicated that he should be off.

'My dear!' The woman elbowed him out of the way and smiled at me with blackened teeth. 'Are you new to London?'

'Well, yes, I am,' I said, 'but I am quite able to look after myself, thank you very much.' I took Betsy's hand firmly in my own, for I had heard of these women who preyed upon unsuspecting newcomers to London, offering them a place to stay while procuring them for immoral purposes, and I did not intend to be a victim.

'Such pretty country looks!' she said, pinching my cheek. 'Such lovely waves in your hair! Have you somewhere to stay, my dear?'

'Yes, I –' I started, but Betsy had let go of my hand and was reaching to pat the two small dogs of a woman who had just stepped from a sedan. 'Betsy!' I called, and grabbed her hand again.

Two peddlers approached, one holding a tray of sweet-meats, one a tray of dolls. An old woman came up close and waved a set of playing cards under my nose, offering to tell my fortune, and a man in rags came a-begging, tapping along with a white stick and bumping into me.

'You must take care,' said the stout man, seemingly reluctant to leave us.

'Really, I am perfectly all right,' I said to him, turning from the woman and waving away the peddlers. 'I have the address of my lodgings and shall go there forthwith. I thank you for your concern.' Still holding on tightly to Betsy, I bent down to pick up the leather bag.

But when I lifted the fur rug, it had gone.

Chapter Ten

'**M**y travelling bag!'

I felt ill, cold and shocked. I hadn't fallen prey to highwaymen and I'd survived the long journey without mishap, but after two minutes in London had been robbed of everything.

I turned, looking frantically behind me. The two peddlers were going in one direction, the blind man shuffling off in another. The old woman was nowhere to be seen, having disappeared into the crowd.

'My dear, have you lost something?' asked the woman with a fan. 'Do allow me to help you search.'

I stared at her. Had she picked up my bag and passed it to someone else? Had the stout man taken it? Or one of the peddlers? Oh, I'd been told often enough that London was a wicked place, full of thieves, beggars and vagabonds, and it certainly was.

I stood still, feeling ghastly sick, not knowing what to do for the best. I wanted to keep standing there until it all came right again. If I wanted it enough, then surely it would be there. The bag couldn't be gone – it *couldn't* be.

But it was.

Betsy tugged at my hand, oblivious to what had happened. 'Can we go and find Will now?'

I swallowed. 'In a moment.'

'My dear?' enquired the woman. 'Do you want me to inform a Bow Street Runner?'

'Fat chance of finding one of those when you want one,' the stout man remarked. 'Besides, who is it he's supposed to be looking for?'

'Go away!' I suddenly shouted – no, screamed – at her, the stout man and anyone else nearby. 'Just please go away and leave us alone!'

Those close by melted away and Betsy, looking at me in horror, burst into tears of fright. I took a deep breath to try and gather myself, then picked up the rug in one arm, took Betsy in the other and began to make my way to the Golden Cross Inn at the back of the vast square where we were standing. On the way, weaving in and out of carriages, people and horses, we passed three men locked into a pillory, which fascinated Betsy so much that she stopped crying.

We reached the wooden boardwalk outside the tavern and I put Betsy down and tried to catch my breath. Together we looked out upon all the hectic misery that was London.

'Why are those men locked in that wooden thing?' Betsy asked.

'I don't know,' I said, too distracted to formulate a proper reply.

'Why have they got their heads and arms through a hole?'

What was I going to do?

'Why is one of them crying?'

'Because they've been very naughty,' I said at last.

'Why are people shouting at them and throwing stuff – oh, someone's thrown a *cat* at them! That's not very nice, is it? Why have they done that?'

'Because . . . because . . .' But I started weeping then, and could not answer.

I had no handkerchief, for such things had been in the bag, so had to dab at my eyes with the edge of my sleeve. What to do? *What to do?*

Darkness was falling, I had no money and thus could not pay for us to stay anywhere. I had a five-year-old child who was dependent upon me, I had lost my mistress's bag, her money and the addresses and could not fulfil the mission for which I'd been sent to London. Oh, I was surely ruined!

At length, while Betsy still gazed, fascinated, at the poor souls in the pillory, I stopped weeping and began to think of possible remedies to my problems. Would I, perhaps, be able to persuade a hackney-cab driver to take us straight back home and rely on the kindness of Miss Alice to pay my fare when I got there? I shook my head at this: I was not brave enough to ask one of those stern, uniformed men for such a favour, for what might I have to do in return? And supposing Miss Alice would not pay when we got there? Perhaps, then, I could find Will as I'd planned, hand over Betsy and ask him or a member of his family to loan me the fare home. Either way, of course, I would be going back without Miss Alice's precious volumes – and she would be sure to think that I'd stolen the money she'd entrusted to me. Besides, although I could hunt for Will, how long would searching for him take – and what would we do for lodgings and food until we found him?

I heaved an enormous sigh and tried to organise my thoughts. Betsy and I were both very tired, but if we walked towards St Paul's Cathedral then perhaps – if we were very lucky – we might actually find Will, or someone who knew him. If we did not, then . . . then I would pawn the travelling rug to raise enough money to rent a room, and carry on our search for Will the next day. My thoughts ran on: once I'd handed Betsy over to him, I might be able to obtain a live-in job in a dairy for two or three weeks. London wages were the best in the country, everyone knew that, so maybe I could even earn enough not only to pay for my journey back home but to buy Miss Alice's book. Yes, this was definitely the best thing, I thought, and I straightened up, brushed myself down and tidied Betsy. I told her, my voice wobbling only slightly, that I had lost our big bag but we were still going to find Will. That it was going to be all right.

I lifted her up so that she could see over the tops of the carriages. 'Look. Do you see that big lead dome?' I said. 'That's the top of this very special church called St Paul's Cathedral. Will lives near there, and that's where we're going.'

Betsy nodded solemnly. 'And will I have cousins to play with?'

'Of course,' I said, 'lots of cousins. And they are town children so you'll be able to teach them all how to make corn dollies.'

I shook out the rug, folded it and put it over my shoulder. It should, I thought, be worth at least three shillings at a pawnshop. I stopped what I was doing for a moment and hesitated: there was something at the back of my mind which was niggling me, but I couldn't quite think what it might be.

All along the Strand it niggled, while we walked on, staring, amazed, at the vast houses and beautiful gardens, at the fashionably dressed ladies going hither and thither in their sedan chairs and carriages, at the men bowing and preening. We went down Fleet Street towards Ludgate Circus and then up the slope to Ludgate Hill, from where we could see the vast, two-tiered, pillared front of St Paul's. We entered an enormous square thronged with peddlers and sightseers and suddenly the whole of the cathedral was visible to us.

Oh, such a place! We just stood and stared and stared at it in awe, and it seemed to me like four churches, built two by two, with, right at the very top, a fifth church, miraculously round, high up in the sky. Upon the leaded dome of this highest church was a golden orb bearing a gold cross.

'Is that *all* St Paul's Cathedral?' Betsy asked after a long moment.

I nodded. 'It is.'

'What is a cathedral?' she asked.

'It's a church. A very special big church.'

'And do people go there on Sundays?'

'If they want to say their prayers, they can go in whenever they like. There are lovely big coloured windows in there, and treasures and wonderful statues.'

'And does Will go? And can we go in, too?'

I hesitated, looking at the crowds thronging the marble steps and at the people going in and out of the huge carved doors for evensong. I shook my head, for I wouldn't have been brave enough to go through those vast doors into the glittering interior I could glimpse within. 'I don't think it's for the likes of us,' I said.

'Why not? Does the King go there?'

'I believe so. When he is well enough.'

'I should like to see the King.'

'He is mad at the moment,' I said – indeed, I couldn't remember a time when he hadn't been mad. 'But at least you can say you have seen his church.'

And it was then that I realised what had been troubling me since I'd arrived: Will had told me that his family lived in view of the cathedral, but I knew now that that great and magnificent dome, so gigantic, so imposing, could be seen for miles around, both on this side of the river and the other. It had been in view, in fact, ever since we'd entered London. And about how many people might live in this huge area and be able to see at least a part of it? A thousand? Two thousand? No, it must be many, many more. Thousands upon thousands. Maybe that impossible number: a million. For St Paul's, built on a hill, loomed above everything and rose high into the sky to touch heaven. So amidst the teeming hundreds and thousands of people how was I ever going to find Will?

Suddenly, I became perfectly certain that I never would. I was on a wild goose chase and I had brought poor little Betsy along with me.

Shocked, I stopped walking, but Betsy let go of my hand and darted off, running up the sweep of stone steps leading to the doors, so that I had to put thoughts of Will to one side, hitch up my skirts and run after her. The crowds of people were so great, and she so tiny, that I knew she could disappear in an instant.

I caught her just before she went through the doors and insisted that she held my hand. We walked all the way round the outside of the vast structure, but now, cast down, I was not just viewing the wonderful statues and the coloured glass windows telling stories from the Bible, but also seeing the pigeon mess, the dead dog lying on a pile of rubbish and the assorted beggars – lacking a leg, an arm, or with sightless eyes or gruesome sores – sitting on the steps and pleading for alms. Betsy surveyed these beggars with interest and occasionally stopped to stare and ask questions: How does the one with no legs walk? Does the blind one fall over? How can the one with no arms eat? It was getting dark now, though, so after a few moments I hurried her on. Where I was actually going, I didn't know, except that I hoped that somehow I might come across Will or see a mention of his family name. Up and down lanes and alleyways we went, through courts, markets, past taverns, gin shops, rickety lodging houses and churches, with me looking into each person's face and not finding Will's likeness in any of them. As every new passageway came into sight Betsy would set up a plaintive cry of 'Is it here that Will lives? Is this his house?', until I became too miserable to respond.

As darkness fell, the peddlers began to disappear from the streets and the poorer sorts of shops, unable to afford a penny candle to light their stock, locked their doors. Our feet were beginning to drag, we were hungry and tired, and Betsy demanded to be picked up then set up a wailing when I said I was too weary to carry her. Still I could not think of what I was going to do; I only knew that I couldn't walk around the streets for ever. Forcing myself to make a decision, I went into the next pawn-broker's I came to and asked for some money to be advanced on Miss Alice's rug.

'It's excellent fur and hardly used,' I said, smoothing it out along the counter. 'It comes from a very well-to-do, titled family.'

The man behind the counter fetched a lit candle and held it over the rug. 'And you *borrowed* it from them, did you?'

I looked at him steadily. His face was grimy, his teeth broken and blackened, and his breath so foul that I felt like recoiling in disgust. I reminded myself, however, that I was only going to pawn a rug to him, not walk out with him. 'No, it was given to me by my mistress,' I said firmly. 'A titled lady.'

'Yers, of course it was.' He looked at Betsy. 'This your little girlie?'

'No, she's my sister,' I said.

He grimaced. 'Yers. Of course.'

But I did not care enough about what he thought of me to press the matter. He offered a shilling for the rug, then I asked for five and we haggled for some minutes, for it seemed to be a mark of honour to him that every penny up or down must be negotiated at length. In the end, with Betsy now lying on the grimy counter, asleep, we settled on two shillings and five pence.

'And could you please tell me if there is a lodging house nearby?' I asked as he counted out the money.

'Lodging house? They's ten a penny round here,' he said. 'Mrs Elm is on the corner, Mr Carpenter three doors down, Mrs . . .'

I moved away, out of reach of his breath. 'And are they quite decent places?'

He smirked, nodding towards Betsy. 'You don't want anywhere too decent, do you? None of the most respectable places will take a single girlie with a child.'

'But I told you – she's not mine!' I protested. 'She's my sister.'

'Yers. So you said.'

I picked up the money. 'There is one other thing I'd like to ask,' I said. 'Are there many watermen around here?'

'Not here!' he said. 'The watermen is all on the river.'

'I know they *work* on the river,' I said, 'but as it's just nearby I thought maybe some might live around here.'

He shrugged. 'Who knows? We've got all sorts.' He ticked them off on his fingers. 'Quacks, peddlers, fruit sellers, washerwomen, drunks, thieves and vagrants.' He tapped his nose. 'And those without any trade at all who must live by their wits and so will starve to death a little quicker than the others.'

Sighing, I was about to pick Betsy up from the counter when I heard a familiar, beloved sound: the faint mooing of a cow, which somehow calmed and reassured me, for I felt that if London had cows in it, then it could not be all bad.

'Is there a dairy round here?' I asked the pawnbroker.

'There's a cow-keeper over yonder,' he said, jerking his thumb backward. 'Mr Holloway. Down the alley and through the iron gates. None too clean.'

I thanked him, my spirits lifting just slightly. I would not attempt to speak to the cow-keeper now, for I was so tired I knew I wouldn't give a good account of myself. I would wait until the next day, and maybe – if I was lucky – obtain a little work.

Chapter Eleven

Opening my eyes the next morning, I had difficulty at first in remembering where I was. Things had happened so quickly: one minute I was living amidst the peaceful calm of the Devonshire countryside, well fed and, I saw now, cushioned from most of life's problems, the next I was fending for myself in alien London, in charge of a child who, dear though she was, was not of my family. Casting my mind hither and thither, my thoughts inevitably came to rest on Will. How could he do this to us? I still wanted to find him – oh, desperately wanted to find him – if only to berate him for the miserable squalor and hopeless predicament that Betsy and I found ourselves in. Everything was his fault! But then, after I'd raged and fumed for some time, it suddenly came to me that I ought to take some of the blame. Will had left us, certainly, but I need not have come to London to search for him. And I definitely should not have brought Betsy with me.

The previous evening it had not taken me long to find lodgings, for once I looked properly I saw that many doors had notices on scraps of paper advertising rooms to let for a respectable family, a tidy single person or a clean couple. Many notes used the words 'respectable' or 'decent' in their requirements for tenants, though I could not help but wonder if the rooms offered lived up to such a description, for in all cases the houses looked dirty and dilapidated, as if they might fall over in a high wind.

Not wishing to go far from the comforting sound of the cow's mooing, and both of us being too tired to walk far, I soon came across a substantial lodging house of six storeys next to a tavern named the Dog and Duck.

The landlord of the lodging house, a Mr Burroughs, proved to be an old man seated in the kitchen before a fire, his boots and stockings off and his large, hairy feet stretched up to the mantelpiece. I was a little nervous in case he should ask anything about Betsy and her connection to me, but he hardly glanced our way, just took my money (two nights at sixpence a night) and said we should go up to the front room on the top floor where we would find a fine chamber awaiting us.

Betsy was crying with tiredness by this time and the stairs were steep – so much so that we had to go up the last flight on all fours. On reaching the top landing I could make out at least five doors off it, but with no light burning anywhere. In fact, it was so very dark that I had to leave Betsy sitting on the top stair and go down to beg a candle stub from our landlord to see us in. Holding this aloft I saw that one door on the landing was standing open, and gingerly going in I found a small room completely empty of furniture apart from a chair and bed. This, I presumed, was to be ours, and in little more than a minute we were both under the blanket and curled up in that bed fast asleep.

Perhaps, I thought, waking at first light the next morning, it was just as well that I hadn't seen the room clearly the night before, for looking around me I could see that the walls were damp and mouldering, their flaking plaster showing the wooden laths underneath and, 'twixt walls and ceiling, a gap showing a streak of grey sky. The bed, too, left much to be desired; the thin blanket we slept under being patched and smelling of dog, and the mattress cover torn, with clumps of straw sticking through it. Moreover, to judge from the lumps and bumps along my legs and up my arms, it was home to a thriving population of fleas and bedbugs. I shuddered; the barns at Bridgeford Hall provided better accommodation for its animals than we had here!

I kept my hands to my sides, trying not to scratch myself, wondering what the time was. And almost immediately I heard a church bell chime seven times, followed by the striking of four other clocks in quick succession. Seven o'clock! More than two hours later than my usual rising time. What should I do? I was too late for that morning's milking and besides, was reluctant to disturb Betsy, for I knew she would immediately present me with a score of questions that I didn't have answers for.

I lay under that miserable blanket as it gradually grew lighter, listening to the strange noises in the house and shivering both from the cold and from contemplation of our plight. Our situation was dire and I could not but wonder what was going to become of us. I had next to no money, no change of clothes, and my shoes – more used to soft grass than the gravel and cobblestones of London – already had holes in the soles from our walk of the day before. What in the name of heaven could I do? I had no relatives to turn to in London, nor any way of getting a message to my family in Arlington. Even if I could have afforded to buy quill, ink and parchment, my parents had no savings to send me nor any means of sending it. Why, my ma didn't even know I was in London!

I thought of everyone at Bridgeford Hall, who in some ways had been as close as my family. This very morning Miss Alice would be imagining that I was at the publisher's collecting her precious book, Mrs Bonny would be berating the maids and Patience would be ingratiating herself with my dear cows. No one would have the least idea about what had happened to me! When I didn't return on time . . . Well, perhaps they would allow me a few days' grace, thinking that I might have been taken poorly, but they would quickly come to the conclusion that I'd met up with Will and decided to stay in London. Miss Alice would be very angry about her book and her money, of course, and Mrs Bonny and the rest of the maids would express surprise that I'd turned out to be so wicked. After that, life for everyone would go on as usual.

But was there any way I could get back to Bridgeford? Betsy, as I saw it, was my main problem. On my own, I might have stood a good chance of earning my fare back home: I was a strong girl and – if I really had to – could go without meat and sleep on the streets to save money. I could not put a small child through that sort of discomfort, however. And even if I paid for the cheapest sort of accommodation for the two of us, what was I going to do with Betsy all day while I worked? I could employ a minder for her, a little girl of about ten years of age, perhaps, but then *she* would need paying and it would eat into what I could earn.

I must have dozed off for a bit then, because when I opened my eyes it was quite light in the room and Betsy's face was an inch from my own.

'I hear a cow mooing!' she said.

I listened. 'So do I. And this afternoon I'm going to go and find her. Perhaps I can get a job in a dairy and earn some money.'

'But what about finding Will? Where are we going to look? Shall we look today?'

'Well,' I said slowly, 'it may take longer than I thought it would.' And I explained to her about St Paul's

Cathedral being vaster than I'd ever imagined, and how it could be seen by thousands of people – so many more than I'd thought.

She frowned and didn't reply for some moments, then drew a deep breath which made me think she was going to cry. She didn't, though. She said, 'There's a little louse crawling along in your hair', which made me jump straight out of bed, fling open the window and shake my head vigorously into the street.

Getting dressed didn't take very long as we had not undressed the night before, and although the landlord had supplied a chamber pot, there was no washing jug or bowl of water. Going out to a day of frosty sunshine, then, I felt dull and frowsy. Betsy, with her own little bag, was lucky enough to have a change of undershift and some clean kerchiefs in her bag – also the coins which had been given to her by Miss Alice's friends. I took these from her, saying I would look after them.

'But you won't spend them, will you?'

'I might,' I said, 'if we're hungry. It all depends how long it takes us to find Will.'

'But we will find him in the end?'

'Yes. Of course,' I said hastily, for her face was crumpling, ready to cry.

We were both very hungry, so sought out breakfast first, eating a small loaf between us while walking along the streets and marvelling at many sights we had been too late to glimpse the evening before. We saw street entertainers jumping on each other's shoulders, throwing balls in the air or making music. We watched quack doctors bragging of the marvels that their lotions and potions could bring about, listened to balladeers singing the latest songs, heard coster-mongers calling their wares and sellers of walnuts, gin and rat poison trying to out-shout each other. There were a great many people selling goods on the streets and scores of shops, and to country folk like Betsy and me they were a source of great interest and fascina-tion. How I longed to buy some of the things for sale: the pretty coloured hairbands, clips and flowers; the creams and unguents which, the peddlers swore, made skin soft as silk and complexions glow like pearls; the sweetmeats and sugary delicacies, the ballads, beauty patches, jellies and fans that seemed so enticing. Oh, had I had the money in my pocket, there were so many things I could have spent it on!

Betsy and I had walked some distance from our lodgings by then, there being so much to draw us on, but at length we found a public well, where we sat and rested ourselves a while, having been told the water was clean and drinkable. A flock of peddlers descended on us then, cajoling and flattering, but they could probably hear the ring of truth in my voice as I said we had no money, for they soon left us alone.

Rested, and mindful that I was going to be enquiring for work, I asked Betsy if I looked clean and tidy. After surveying me carefully she said I was moderately fine, although I had white dust from the bread on my nose. I remedied this, washed my hands and face at the well and then we set off to retrace our footsteps and locate the source of the mooing.

In spite of the dairy being near to our lodgings it took some finding, for it was in a narrow lane which turned in on itself, leaving a sort of blind alley at the end which was fronted by a large shed-like affair with two rusting doors. I knew the cows must be nearby because there was a mess of stinking milk, mud and straw on the stamped-earth floor. There were also two milk churns standing on a small wheeled trap, so I presumed that whoever owned the dairy must take a delivery to the nearby neighbours. Venturing inside the building I found another, overturned, churn and there was also a milkmaid's wooden yoke with a pail at each end. The whole place, however, stank of rancid milk, rust and mould, and was as different from my sweet-smelling dairy as it was possible to be.

Going further in, the first thing which struck me after the smell was the disarray. Mrs Bonny would have run mad to see it! Cobwebs trailed from grimy corners like raggedy curtains, the paint on the wooden counter had all but peeled off and there was a jumbled collection of ladles, pint pots, skimmers and cream-setting pans along the work surfaces.

''Tis not like *your* dairy!' Betsy said, looking around her in disgust. She crouched down on the floor. 'There are mouse droppings. If I had a little box I could find one and keep it as a pet.'

'Don't let's look for mice now,' I said hastily. Then I called 'Hello!' several times, and Betsy did likewise.

After a considerable time a man with generous sideburns and a moustache appeared from behind the counter, where I presumed he'd been sleeping. This, I thought, must be Mr Holloway, the cow-keeper.

'No more milk today,' he said. 'Try our other place.'

'I don't want to buy milk,' I said.

'Nor butter,' he continued, smoothing down his moustache. 'We've no time here for the churning of butter.'

I shook my head. 'If you please . . . I have recently come from the country,' I said – for word had it that London employers were well disposed to country girls, thinking them more honest than those bred in the city.

'Aye.'

'I'm looking for work. I'm an experienced milkmaid.' I thought I detected a glimmer of interest in his face so went on. 'Until very recently I cared for a small herd of cows in Devonshire, keeping the dairy in good order, milking twice daily and making cream and butter.'

'Done a milk round, have you?' he asked, yawning between his words.

I shook my head.

'I have eight cows. I could do with a girl here some-times . . .'

'After milking the cows I could easily do a round!' I said, gesturing towards the little trap. 'I could manage a small pony.'

He shook his head. 'We don't keep a pony in winter – our cows don't give enough milk to make it worthwhile. You'd have to take the yoke and pails out.'

I nodded again, trying to look keen, although I had heard the girls on the big farm complaining how uncomfortable the yokes were and how their backs ached after walking for even a few minutes with a heavy pail at each end. 'I could do that, sir.'

He scratched his head. 'We've got a second dairy down Soho, way bigger than this. If you were here, then I'd have more time to spend at the other place.'

'I should need a good weekly wage,' I said boldly, then gestured around at the mess. 'But I would get your dairy in proper order.'

He twisted his head to look at Betsy standing behind me. 'Whose bairn is that?'

'She's a . . . a friend's little sister.'

He didn't appear to have heard my words. 'Your child, is she?'

I blushed. 'No, not mine. She is my friend's sister.'

He frowned at Betsy and then – just when I thought he was going to turn me away for not being respectable enough – said, 'A week's trial at five shillings.'

'Ten,' I said promptly.

We settled on seven, and arranged that I should start the following morning at four.

I explained to Betsy that I had to work to earn some money while we searched for Will, and she accepted this quite readily. I would, I said, be going to Mr Holloway's dairy early in the mornings, and that, on waking, she was to stay in bed for as long as possible and only when she couldn't possibly wait any longer should she come round to the dairy to find me. I got a lump in my throat as I said this, thinking that the poor child should be safely at home in a warm kitchen with a family, not stuck in a miserable room for hours on end with no one bar bedbugs for company, but this was the best I could do.

I'd bought some short ends of narrow red ribband, and with these and several lengths of straw taken out of the mattress, told her to make some more corn dollies while she waited. I impressed upon her that, on leaving the lodging house to come and find me, she should come straight round to the dairy and not dilly-dally or speak to anyone. I had already, listening to women in the market, heard of a child who had been taken off the street, stripped of all its good clothes and sent home wearing only its vest. Betsy's little country smock, shawl and shoes were only worth a few pennies, but nevertheless would be valuable to a woman whose child had nothing. I just had to hope and pray that nothing bad would happen to her.

Chapter Twelve

I woke to hear the clocks strike three o'clock and lay awake until I heard a cryer call that it was half past three on a wet morning. Rising, I found the room dismally cold and, although I was used to waking to a freezing room in Bridgeford Hall, *this* cold seemed much worse, because there was no rug on the floor, no shutters at the windows nor a bold patchwork quilt to lift the cheerless scene. I would have liked a clean apron to wear to work, but had not, of course, thought to bring such a thing with me. The evening before I had asked our landlord for a jug and basin, however, so I was at least able to wash myself, and I used Betsy's little scrubbing brush to cleanse my hands and nails thoroughly, just in case my new employer should take it upon himself to inspect them. I was, in spite of the gloom of the morning, looking forward to meeting my new four-legged friends and seeing the extent of my workplace. If I did well there and he kept me on, surely it wouldn't take long for me to earn our fare back to Devonshire.

On leaving the lodging house I had to light a candle in order to see my way through the streets and was very nervous as to where I was putting my feet, for it had rained heavily in the night and much rubbish – offal, mud, dead rats and stinking old green-stuffs – had swept its way down from the higher ground of the fruit and vegetable market and deposited itself into the corners and holes between the cobbles. It had stopped raining, but the ground was very slippery, and twice I fell over on to heaps of soft and squelchy matter, so I fear that when I arrived I was not nearly as clean as when I left.

Going through the rusty gates I could hear, somewhere, two or three cows mooing heartily, so I presumed that the cow stalls were out at the back of the dairy, perhaps with some outside space and a little patch of green grass for them to chew on.

I called, 'Mr Holloway!' then stood and listened through the mooing for a reply. Light was coming in, dimly, from a lantern in the street, which enabled me to see a sconce in the wall of the dairy with a flint box beside it. I lit the candle in the sconce and, while I waited, looked around me. The stink of cows was horrendous; I began to wonder how clean their stalls were, and how good their milk.

'Have you made a start?'

I jumped, alarmed, for the mud was soft underfoot

and I hadn't heard my employer coming up behind me. He stood frowning at me, his face so strangely illuminated by the lantern he carried that he looked like someone dressed as a ghostie for All Hallows' Eve.

'Not yet,' I replied. I looked around. 'Where are the pails and stools?' I asked, then gave a little nervous laugh. 'Where are the *cows*?'

'All down below,' he said, and he gestured into the space beyond. 'They had a bale of straw and a sack o' turnips late last night.'

I looked at him, baffled.

'Get you started, then. They're below, I said.'

'Below?' I repeated. I did not have the slightest notion what he meant. In the lower field, perhaps?

He shook his head. 'Country girls!' he said with some amusement. 'Down the ladder – off you go.' He gave me the lantern. 'I'll be back in a couple of hours. You should be finished by then.'

I didn't say anything in reply to this. Eight cows are not that many for one girl to milk, but the fastest time in which I can milk a cow is ten minutes – and that on a good day when your cow is being quiet and obedient. If she wants to be difficult, then twenty minutes might be more usual, and even up to thirty minutes if you don't know her well and she has a mind to play you up.

Mr Holloway left me, which I was glad about, for I had been afeared he would stay and watch me milking. Lifting the lantern, I tried to see into the darkness below me and took a nervous step forward. Down the ladder, he'd told me. But surely the cows couldn't be down a ladder, *underground*?

But they were. Another two steps forward and I could see a large square hole cut into the floor, like a trapdoor, with a ladder descending from it, and lifting my lantern higher and peering downwards I could see some movement below.

I stood and stared down, scarce able to believe what I was seeing. Cows in the cellar! Why, these poor creatures should be outside enjoying the dawn air while they waited to go into their milking parlour, or at least be in a barn, feeding. How could cows possibly live underground?

I hitched up my skirts, placed the lantern at the top of the hole and climbed down a few steps, then retrieved the lantern and climbed the rest of the way. It was a good job, I thought, that I was used to the smell of cows, although this was not so much a smell as a heady, stomach-wrenching stink. At the bottom of the ladder, crammed into a small space and looking thoroughly miserable, the eight cows were standing in their own filth. They had a manger of turnips to eat, and a bale of hay was hanging about head height, but they were paying little attention to these. At some point someone had made an effort to clear their standing space, for there was a channel affair running around the room and a long-handled broom to brush the muck into, but it made little difference to the overall state of the cellar before me.

I turned my attention to the cows themselves and could have cried at their condition. What a sight they were: crammed together with barely enough space to turn around in, smelly and distressed and stuck all over with muck and mud. How miserable they looked! Why, the poor creatures had probably never rolled in a patch of clover or eaten fresh grass in all their lives. I felt like turning and scrambling back up that ladder as fast as I could, but I knew I had to stay.

Sighing, I surveyed the cows. I was in a quandary now, for the main thing with milking, the first lesson I was ever taught by my mother, was that cleanliness must come first. Nothing else was as important as ensuring that a milkmaid's hands, the hindquarters of the cow and any equipment that was going to come into contact with the milk was as clean as could be, or otherwise all sorts of infections and illnesses could be spread. I had no access here to hot water, however, and no way of knowing if the pails I could see standing about had been scoured and aired, or the churns cleaned with wood ash and then scalded. I thought it was highly unlikely.

For the sake of the cows I wanted to do the best I could, so I went back up the ladder and out on to the street, filled a pail with water from the nearest pump and took it back down. I then went up and down the ladder several times for clean water, so that half an hour passed before I had even started the milking.

After acquainting myself with the cows (I believed,

from what I could see, they were of the Jersey breed), I washed their rear ends with some rags that I'd found hanging on nails, and while doing so spoke to them in a gentle voice, telling them of my lovely South Devons at home, of how Betsy and I had come to be in London and even about the falseness of Will, so that they became used to my voice. People sometimes query the effectiveness of this, but I knew from experience that cows who are spoken to kindly yield more milk than cows where the milkmaid has nothing at all to say for herself or, worse still, is abrupt and offhand.

At last I was ready to begin and though, in that grim little room, it was difficult to find a space where a girl could sit and milk quietly and not be kicked by the next cow in line, eventually I found a corner, picked what I thought to be the cow in most urgent need of being milked, rinsed out the bucket and started.

The quality of the milk yielded was poor; I could see that straight away. It was thin and blue-looking rather than creamy in texture and colour. And although, of course, cows give less milk in the winter, I barely got a full pail from the first one I tried. The others gave about the same and I knew the truth of the expression that miserable cows give miserable portions.

Mr Holloway arrived down the ladder – thankfully much later than he had predicted – just as I was finishing.

'Is this all you have from 'em?' he asked, holding a candle aloft over the line of buckets.

'Indeed it is – and you're lucky to have it!' I said, for by this time I had roused myself into a ball of indignation about the cows and the conditions in which they lived.

''Tis a wretched small amount.'

'And 'tis a wretched life for these cows – standing around in their own muck day after day with ne'er a sight of the sun,' I retorted. I went on, surprised at my own boldness. 'It's a wonder that they haven't dried up entirely.'

He shrugged, and it was strange to me that, whereas I would have taken it personally if someone criticised my cows and the way they were kept, he didn't seem to be bothered either way. 'These are London cows born and bred,' he said. 'That's the way of cows 'ere.'

'But they need air and light and grass!'

'They get their turnips and their good hay. Why, some days in winter they cost more to feed than they gives.'

'But do they ever go outside?'

'Not they!' he said. 'They come in, they're lowered down on ropes and there they stay until they dry up or die.' He looked interested suddenly. 'But in the country, surely your beasts aren't out all year round?'

'They stay under cover in really bad weather,' I said, 'but most winter days they are turned out to nibble the grass and take a little air.'

'Take a little air!' He began laughing. 'Seems to me that cows in Devonshire lead an altogether daintier life than those in London!'

'I believe they do,' I said, and might have gone on to tell him of Miss Alice and Miss Sophia's pastoral *tableau*, except that I heard Betsy's voice from above, calling my name.

'I'll go and do the round now, shall I?' I asked Mr Holloway quickly, before he could comment on Betsy. 'Where must I go?'

She shouted again, saying that she had made six corn dollies and had no more ribband left, and he glanced upwards and looked curious, but didn't say anything. I called back that I would come up in a moment, and prayed that she wouldn't wander off.

'My milk round is at the other end of the Strand,' he said. 'I have twenty or more houses with an H chalked on the wall – that means they have credit with me. If you call outside them, a housemaid will come down with a jug.'

I nodded. The Strand was, I knew, some fair distance off, for we had walked all the way down it after arriving at Charing Cross. 'I must take the yoke and pails?' I asked.

He nodded, then gave a humourless grin. 'But afore you go, you must visit the cow with the iron tail.'

'*Which* cow?' I asked.

He gave a snort of laughter. ''Tis what we cow-keepers in London call the water pump.'

I still did not know what he was talking about. 'To wash the pails?'

'No, to dampen the milk!'

'*Dampen?*' I repeated.

'The milk is too rich for most of our customers. Too thick, too creamy. Give 'em indigestion, it would.'

'Would it?' I asked in surprise, for, newly up from the country, I believed what I was told.

'It goes further when 'tis damped down,' he said, grinning. 'Sometimes it goes near twice as far.'

And then, of course, I realised what he was talking about. The milk, even though it was poor quality, was to be diluted before it was sold.

'You water it down?'

'Hush!' he said. 'But not with river water,' he added virtuously, 'for once I had complaints that there was a fish in the milk.'

I stared at him in dismay.

'No, you must use water from the pump,' he said. 'A quarter-pail of water to every pail of milk. I'll go and fetch it now.'

He went up and we 'damped' the milk down and I did not approve in the slightest, but merely wondered how many more London ways I would have to get used to.

Betsy and I walked along Fleet Street towards the Strand, and the distance seemed far greater now that I had a yoke over my shoulders with a pail of milk balanced on each end. These pails were not lidded, but open to the elements so that anyone might spit or cough over them, or apprentice boys could, for sport, choose to throw in a handful of dirt.

Betsy was scratchy and tired and determined to be

difficult. She wouldn't hold on to my hand, but kept stopping and looking in windows or sitting down on the cobbles to talk to passing cats and dogs. I would alternately shout at her, plead with her, try to bribe her – but, of course, with a great wooden yoke across my shoulders I often couldn't move quickly enough to catch hold of her. In the end I had to promise her faithfully that, as soon as I had delivered all the milk, we would go down to the river and look for Will. She was cold, I knew, and hungry, too, for although we'd had some undiluted milk to drink (and trusted to luck that it would not be tainted), other than that we'd had nothing.

We both needed to eat. Worried about money, I reckoned up the price of things in my head: I had pawned the fur rug for two shillings and five pence, our room for two nights had been a shilling, so, after taking off the cost of the food we'd had the previous day, there should now be one shilling and sixpence in my pocket (although I could not, of course, check this because of trying to keep the yoke balanced). This would pay for two more nights' lodging. But we had to eat right at that moment, for it was near noon and Betsy was trailing behind me again, crying, so I stopped a pieman and bought a meat pasty. I gave Betsy the biggest half, tried to stop her tears and sighed mightily as I did so, for I had discovered that having a child with you was a very great burden and that I was not really up to it. I loved her very much, I was sorry for what she was having to go through, but also felt sorry for myself and longed not to have the responsibility of her.

By the time I found the first house marked with an H, my back felt as if it were breaking. As I walked along, I shifted the yoke around on my shoulders, first leaning it one way, then the other, then putting both my hands up and underneath it to help bear its weight, but whatever I did brought little relief.

'Milk below!' I called up to the houses. 'Fresh milk below!'

I knew I must look a sight, for I was grubby and tired, with bird's-nest hair and cheeks cracking under smudges of dried milk. So much for the pretty pastoral scene depicted by Miss Alice and Miss Sophia, I thought. So much for the May Day milkmaids, garlanded with flowers, dancing along the street to a fiddler's tune. I knew the truth now.

By calling 'Milk below!' under the windows of those houses marked with a chalked H, I sold all the milk in my pails quite quickly. Though I had to get back for that afternoon's milking, I'd promised Betsy that we would go and look for Will, so didn't think it would hurt to go back the slightly longer way, by the river path.

Walking down Clover Street, the stink of the river hit us as soon as we were no longer sheltered by buildings, and this odour increased the closer we came to the water, even though it had rained the night before and washed most of the sewage and garbage away on the tide. I thanked heaven that it was a cold month, too, for as I'd walked along Fleet Street I'd heard a woman say that in high summer the river smelled so bad it could make a grown man fall down insensible.

Once we had stopped gagging at the stench, there was much to stare at: steamboats, barges laden with grain or coal, little boats with sails, wherries, sailing ships with cargo aboard, and even one or two grand barges bearing the flags and insignia of livery companies. Most numerous of all, however, were the ferry boats darting backwards and forwards laden with passengers, with those who rowed them shouting and hollering at other, larger boat-owners, who hollered right back.

So much to see; so many ferry boats. How was I ever going to find Will amongst them?

I stood there, bewildered, my eyes criss-crossing the river to the far side and back again, trying to count how many little boats there were going backwards and forwards. This was a hopeless task, I soon realised, akin to trying to count the number of cherries on a tree.

There was an old sailor close by us, in dark oilskin and a sou'wester, and I waited until he'd finished puffing on his pipe, then asked if he knew how many ferrymen there were on the river.

'Just roughly,' I added. 'Would it be about . . . one hundred?'

'One hundred!' he said scornfully. 'Pssshh! I could see one hundred with my eyes shut. No, there must be nigh on a thousand. Probably more.'

I stared at him in dismay.

'Ferry boats is like ants all over the river and back again,' he said, gesturing with his arms. 'Why, there are so many ferrymen with so many boats that sometimes a fellow has to wait half an hour at Puddle Dock for a landing space.'

My heart sank. '*That* many ferries?'

Betsy was hanging over the river wall and not listening to us, so I felt safe to ask him, in a low voice, if he might possibly know of the Villiers family, who were ferrymen born and bred.

He shook his head.

'They have a cousin who has lately joined them from the country,' I added as a desperate afterthought, but he just grunted and began refilling his pipe.

Betsy straightened up, sighed and yawned. 'Oh, where *is* Will?' she said crossly. 'I'm getting tired of him not being here.'

'So am I,' I answered miserably.

'When are we going to find him?'

I shook my head. 'I don't know. You see, we don't know which stretch of water he works on. The Thames is a big, big river.'

I decided to tell her – for I thought I should introduce the idea as soon as possible – that we might not be able to find Will. 'He could be anywhere.' I looked at her carefully, trying to judge her mood. 'We might not find him. We might have to go home and wait for him to come back to us.'

'But you said he . . .'

'I didn't realise how big London was, Betsy.'

'I hate Will!' she suddenly cried. 'I do! We both hate him, don't we?'

'Hush, no, of course we don't,' I said, but there was no conviction in my voice.

Chapter Thirteen

I carried on for several days at Mr Holloway's, being paid daily. I milked twice a day (thankfully, my milk round in the afternoons was shorter and closer) and between times endeavoured to get the cows, churns and milk pails as clean as I could. After only three days, I was pleased to see that the cows all began to yield a little more milk and, though Mr Holloway did not actually comment on this, he did nod and look pleased when I told him.

Some of what remained of the milk was sold to people who came to the door of the dairy, and the rest was taken away by Mr Holloway. I did no churning of butter nor making of cream or cheese during this time: there was never enough milk. Besides, Mr Holloway told me that those living in the nearby tenements could not have afforded such items. Over those days I grew to know my cows a little, for when your cheek is pressed up against the warm flank of an animal for twenty minutes or so, you do come to feel a kind of understanding between you. The duty I very much disliked was the diluting of milk with water, for I'd long believed that the milk's quality was dependent on how happy the cows were, and that a miserably thin liquid showed badly on both stock-keeper and milkmaid. Those finer feelings, however, had to be pushed to one side for the time being, for I knew I had to go along with London ways if I was going to survive.

Betsy was nearly always at my side, and I was constantly trying to keep her occupied in one way or another. My life had become a struggle and I sometimes felt as though I was one of the street jugglers, trying to keep ten coloured balls in the air at once. When I was not milking, or scrubbing and scouring, or walking along the road under the weight of the yoke, I was trying to keep Betsy from running off, telling her tales to try to amuse her or cajoling, chastising or pleading with her.

On what should have been my seventh day of employment at the dairy, something awful happened: Betsy became ill. She woke in the small hours vomiting – an action that was so strange and alien to her that it made her scream in fright between bouts. I was kept busy comforting her, running up and down the stairs fetching water, cleaning up, emptying the chamber pot into the closet in the yard and returning it to the room for the next attack. At one point, the poor child made so much noise in her panic that our neighbours in the next rooms banged on the door and shouted at us – not to offer help, but to bring down curses on our heads for disturbing them. I was very frightened at all this, and felt I could not cope, for we had been a healthy bunch in the country and I had little to no experience of disease or illness. Terrified, I wondered what would happen if I caught this malaise as well. Who would look after us?

As the clocks struck four o'clock that morning I was wide awake and worried. Betsy was not vomiting so much, but lay shivering on the bed under the weight of all the clothes we possessed while I, lying on the edge of the bed and freezing cold in my undershift, stroked back her hair from her face and made soothing noises. I did not know what to do. I had to go to work – my cows would be waiting for me and unless I worked I couldn't afford to pay for the room – but how could I possibly leave Betsy? What if she became worse? What if she died?

With this thought uppermost in my head, I began weeping. I should never have brought her with me! I should have come to London alone, run my errand for Miss Alice and then gone home. On my own, I surely wouldn't have been so distracted as to lose that bag. To think that I'd been so naive to believe that, amidst all the thousands of people in London, I'd find Will! Especially, I thought now for the first time, if he didn't want to be found . . .

*

I must have fallen asleep again because daylight was showing through the thick frost on the windows by the time I rose. I thought about how I felt: was I sick or aching? Was my throat or head hurting? The answer to all these questions was no, so I carefully took my shawl off the bed and wrapped it around me, then examined Betsy. She was sleeping, pale and still, but I could not tell if it was a healthy sleep or one of total exhaustion. Her hair was stuck around her face and sweat beaded her brow, yet her body remained cold and her fingers and toes were tinged with blue.

I shivered and sighed, scratching on the window to try and see through the layer of frost to the street below. By now, of course, Mr Holloway would realise that I hadn't turned up to milk the cows. I should have gone and explained things to him, but was too scared to leave Betsy – and too nervous about what Mr Holloway might say. I felt sorry for my cows when I thought about him discovering them unmilked and, cross and heavy-handed, taking the pail to them himself, but there was nothing I could do about it.

I could only remember one piece of advice from my mother regarding health matters and that was to feed a cold and starve a fever, but this was of little help now, for I was not sure if Betsy had either or both. I thought back, but couldn't remember any of my brothers or sisters being sick enough to stay in bed – although we had all had the spotted fever, of course . . .

Remembering this, I peeled back the coverings on Betsy and looked for spots, but there were none. The blanket was damp and cold from where I'd tried to sponge it clean, however, and when I moved it Betsy shivered in her sleep and wrapped her arms around herself, whimpering, so I knew I must try to warm her.

Carefully I removed my clothes from the bed and got dressed. I had errands to run: I must buy wood and perhaps coal for the fire, purchase some food, and also ask at an apothecary's for a cordial or powder to help Betsy. I looked in my pocket: I had a few coins, but – now that I wasn't working – when they were gone, absolutely no means of getting more.

I checked on Betsy again and again as I was tidying myself to go out, nervous about leaving her, then crept down the stairs, luckily not meeting any of those we shared the house with. I turned in the direction of St Paul's rather than go near to Mr Holloway's.

The wood was easy to buy, for almost every shop sold bundles of firewood, but I was shocked at the price of coal and decided we must manage without it. At a fish stall, I bought the very cheapest of fish: four sprats for a penny, which I intended to cook on the open fire, and spent another penny for some bread to help the bones go down. I did not manage so well in the apothecary's shop, however. The one I visited was near to the cathedral, heavily scented with herbs and well lit by both candles and oil lamps. A lady dressed in purple silk with a white fur jacket was there wanting to purchase something with which to wash her hair, and the two gentleman assistants were so engrossed in discussing, searching for and weighing out what she wanted from the bulbous jars that, although I coughed a few times, they took no notice of me at all.

I waited patiently for some moments and then tried a tentative 'Excuse me', which was ignored. I tried again and then, feeling my face reddening with embarrassment, backed slowly towards the door. When I reached it, I flung it open and ran for home, hearing and ignoring a commanding call from behind me of 'Close the door, if you please!'

I walked along, furious and tearful, but then caught sight of my reflection in a shop window. Why, with my dress stained and mud splattered, my face unwashed and hair tangled, I looked like the poorest sort of beggar.

I sighed heartily. Beggar I would be soon enough.

I might have stopped at one of the quack doctors for a tincture for Betsy, but I was in too much of a hurry to get back to her. Besides, the first quack I passed had a big crowd about him and was in the middle of a shouted tirade against the wickedness of all apothecaries and surgeons and did not seem about to stop. One other man, who had set up a table inside the wide doorway of a tavern, was wearing the mask of a wild animal and was roaring at passers-by to emphasise that his medicine would make you as strong as a lion. He was doing this with such vigour, however, that I was frightened to approach him.

Thus I had to trust that Betsy's malaise was nothing serious and would go in its own good time.

Chapter Fourteen

I hurried back to the lodging house with the newspaper-wrapped parcel of sprats under my arm, hoping that Betsy wouldn't have woken up and wondering how I was going to cook the fish. I knew how to make little dishes from milk: puddings, custards and flummeries, but I had never before cooked fish or meat. I'd seen a little trivet affair standing in front of the grate in our room and intended to place the fish on this so it could be smoked by the fire.

Suddenly realising that Betsy must have something to drink, I asked a passer-by and was directed to a proper dairy just off the Strand. This had a brass engraving above the door naming it the Nell Gwyn Dairy and saying it had been there since the days of Charles II. A card in the window respectfully informed the public that their freshly churned butter could be made into ornamental figures and that, although no cows were kept on the premises, fresh milk was delivered from the country twice a day. The shop stood, glossily tiled and painted, to serve the magnificent houses around Whitehall – and was as different from Mr Holloway's dairy as it was possible for a place to be. The milk I purchased here was, of course, a much better colour and consistency than that offered by his animals, for I could see it had not been tampered with. It was quite costly, though, being one penny for a small can.

The front door of the lodging house was standing open when I arrived back, and I stepped in as lightly as possible, for I owed Mr Burroughs for my lodging charges. I'd only put one foot on the bottom stair, however, when I heard him shout, 'You come along here, girl!' and I had no alternative but to go in to him. He was in the first room of the house, as he had been before, lying back in a rocking chair with his gnarled feet on the mantelpiece.

'You owe me money, I b'lieve.'

I nodded. 'I do. I was just about to come and give it to you.'

He gave a mocking laugh. 'Were you indeed?'

'I was!' I delved into my pocket and brought out a shilling. 'That's for last night and tonight,' I said. I did some sums in my head. I had just enough left to pay for one more night's lodging and some food for the following day, but after that we would be penniless. Surely Betsy would be better by then and I could go and find a way of earning more money?

'That's not enough,' said Mr Burroughs. 'The price has gone up.'

'But . . . why?'

'That's a lovely room you've got – too good for sixpence. Should be eight.'

'But I haven't got that much.'

He shrugged. 'And you've been disturbing my other guests in the night. They're threatening to go elsewhere, and if they do I shall set their lodging charges at your door.'

'But last night we couldn't help it – the little girl with me was sick!' I protested.

He shrugged again. 'What's that to me?'

'She was frightened because we haven't ever been away from home before,' I said, hoping to soften his heart. 'My mistress sent me from the country to collect a newly published book, and our portman-teau –'

'Got took as soon as you arrived,' he finished, to my great astonishment. 'Or was carried orf by a highway-man. Or fell orf the top of the coach. And now you can't pay your way. I've heard it all before.'

'But it's true!'

''Course it is,' he snorted. 'You girls come up from the country believing that a pretty face is going to work miracles. Think you're going to snare a rich patron, don't you? Well, it won't work for me! And let me tell you now that I won't have anything of a doubtful nature going on in my rooms.'

I knew what he was referring to and felt very affronted. 'I can tell you now I would not dream of –'

'You come to London with your bastard child, to a respectable, God-fearing house, and think to use my honest lodgings as a place of dalliance.'

I was tearful and enraged by this time and longed to retaliate, but did not dare do so in case he threw us out on to the street. I took a deep breath. 'Then rest assured I will leave here as soon as I am able, and find somewhere more suitable to a well-brought-up girl and her charge.'

He snorted.

'I will leave tomorrow.'

'Not afore you've paid me what you owe me,' he said, turning back to his contemplation of the fire. 'One shilling and four pence.'

I was absolutely furious, yet I had no alternative but to pay him even though it pained me deeply to do so. I now had tuppence left in the world.

My heart was in my mouth when I pushed open our door, but all was quiet in there. The rancid smell of sickness hung in the room, however, and it was so cold that my breath puffed out in front of me like steam as I went to check how Betsy was. Finding her very pale and still sleeping, I became frightened that she might have fallen into some sort of coma, so woke her. I regretted this immediately, of course, for she began weeping high and loud, saying that she wanted to go home.

I sat on the bed, put my arms around her and rocked her. 'Everything will be all right. You'll feel better tomorrow and then we'll start looking for Will again,' I said.

'I'll get a fire going now and then I'm going to cook our dinner. You'd like that, wouldn't you?'

I laid up a fire with the sticks and a little of the newspaper and, with the help of an old tinderbox left in the grate, managed to get it alight. I talked to Betsy all the time as I did so, shushing and singing to try and cheer her, telling her of all the people I'd seen when I'd been out, of the gown worn by the aristocratic woman in the apothecary's, of the quack doctor with his animal mask, of the bill I'd seen advertising a troupe of singing mice. Inside, however, I was feeling quite desperate. I loved Betsy, but felt ill equipped to cope with her. If I had been the eldest in our family it might have been better, for I would have been well versed in the ways of infants and their wants and needs, but I was the youngest of nine and so had no practice.

When the fire was going reasonably well I put the sprats on the trivet to cook them but, once they were smoked through, found they were stubbornly stuck on to the metal grill affair. I had to scrape them off, so they didn't look very appetising, but, after carefully picking out the bigger bones, we ate them as best we could with some bread. Despite my encouraging her every mouthful, Betsy only ate a pitifully small amount. While I chewed on the ill-tasting pieces of fish (there was a reason they were four for only a penny) I tested myself constantly as to how I felt: did I feel nauseous, giddy or faint; did my limbs or my head ache? What I feared most was that I would catch whatever malaise

Betsy had and become desperately ill. Following this, Betsy (so my imagination ran) would be quite unable to fend for herself and so have a relapse, then we would both die and the wicked landlord would discover our bodies some days later. Would our sad demise be in the London papers, I wondered? Would Will get to hear of it?

When I could not persuade Betsy to eat any more, I told her to lie down and close her eyes. Going to tuck the blanket around her, I found it still damp, so I shook it out and put it over the chair in front of the fire to air. I then wrapped Betsy tightly in both her shawl and my own to keep her warm. She smiled a little at this, but did not speak, seeming to have no strength left in her. She had stopped vomiting, however, and I thought that this was a good sign. I poked the fire so that a flame sprung up, but without coal there was no hot centre to the fire and the flimsy sticks of wood were being eaten quickly by the flames, burning one after the other as fast as I could put them on. How short-sighted I'd been; I should have bought two bundles!

I looked at Betsy: she was sleeping well enough, but I couldn't go out and leave her with a fire burning only a foot or two away. I didn't want to wait until the fire had gone right out, though, because it had taken me many minutes to get it started.

The flames burned lower, the wooden sticks charring, then crumbling to nothing, until I had just four pieces of wood left. Outside I heard the clocks striking noon – dinner hour – and the cries of the piemen and hot-potato men to 'Come buy!' increased in number and volume. How I would have loved a hot potato, perhaps with a smear of my dairy butter and a little of Mrs Bonny's best cheese on top. But I tried to put this thought from my mind.

I left the addition of each of the remaining sticks of firewood until the last possible moment, until there was just one left. After putting these on, I rolled up the remains of the fish – all the bones and heads – in the newspaper they'd been wrapped in and burned that, and as this spurt of flames died away, looked around the room for something else. We had nothing suitable: no spare clothes, no spare anything. Our shoes would have burned well, but we certainly could not do without them.

My glance fell on the one chair in the room. It was a shabby enough thing: an old kitchen chair with a rush seat, battered and rickety, its joints loose.

Could I?

It was surely not worth more than a penny or two. Besides, the landlord would probably not even know it had gone until we'd left the house.

Undecided, I waited until my last piece of wood had almost burned through, then picked up the chair and shook it a little, just to see what would happen . . . to see whether it was ready to be broken up. I found that it was, for it only took a couple of shakes for one of the spurs holding the legs in place to fall out.

I left it lying on the floor while I thought about it, until Betsy gave a shuddering, shivering sob in her sleep which near broke my heart. I touched her face; she was still icy cold. People could die of being cold, I knew that; every winter we'd hear about one or two travelling beggars who'd frozen to death in the hedges.

I put the wooden spur from the chair on the fire. The wood, being hard, did not catch immediately, but when it did, it began to throw out merry little flames all along its length.

There was no going back now. I removed all four legs from the chair, wriggled the seat so that the struts holding the cane fell out, then did the same for the backrest. In no time at all, it seemed, the chair was in pieces on the floor in front of me. I moved closer to the fire and began to feed the chair, piece by piece, on to it. As the flames burned up I thought of home, and sitting in front of the fire with my ma and pa on cold nights, as well as the huge marble fire-places at Bridgeford Hall and the great logs they brought in every winter. Mostly, though, I thought of Will and how he'd come up to the big house one evening and, the other servants being already abed, we'd opened the front of the kitchen range and toasted chestnuts on a little brass shovel. How happy we'd been then.

When the cane seat went on to the fire, I felt I wanted to wake Betsy to see the sight, for the cane crackled and sparked and the orange, yellow and blue flames flared and danced, making the whole room light up and giving it an almost cheerful aspect.

I held my hands out to the heat, feeling them warm for the first time in days. If Betsy recovered quickly, I thought, maybe it would still be all right. We could search along the river for Will or members of his family – and perhaps be able to discover a way of earning a little money while we did so. Perhaps, if I made myself presentable, I might even get a job in the beautiful dairy in the Strand.

But as I sat there musing, disaster came – smoke began coming back down the chimney, first creeping into the room and then billowing out in great clouds of acrid black and making me cough.

I jumped up and flapped my skirts at the smoke a bit, not knowing what else to do. There came the sound of heavy feet crashing up the stairs, and Mr Burroughs burst into our room.

'You've set my chimneys on fire!' he shouted. 'You stupid jade! Who said you could have a fire?'

Startled and frightened by his sudden appearance, I didn't reply, merely waved at the smoke to try and disperse it.

'If you wanted a fire you should have paid for a climbing boy to sweep the chimney!'

'I'm sorry. I didn't know,' I said. I glanced at Betsy on the bed: miraculously, she was still asleep. 'But, anyway, I can let the fire go out now.' I stood up and shook out the still damp blanket, more as a distraction than anything else, for I didn't want him to see that his chair was missing.

'If that smoke has blown back into my other rooms, spoiling people's clothes and such . . .'

'I'll pay for the damage,' I said quickly, knowing exactly how much money I had in my purse and thinking that Betsy and I would have to make a run for it. I edged towards the last piece of the chair: the curved back strut which was lying on the floor. If I could just push it under the bed with my foot . . .

'And there's to be no more fires here until –' His glance suddenly fell to the floor. 'What is it that you've been burning?'

Betsy began whimpering in her sleep, then opened her eyes.

'Firewood,' I replied quickly, 'and some newspaper and fish bones.'

'What's that on the floor, then?' He pointed at the chair strut.

'Just firewood,' I answered.

'That's not firewood – that's my chair. My fine dining chair!'

' 'Twas not *fine*!' I said immediately. 'It was an old, broken-down kitchen chair, only fit to be used for a fire.'

He picked up the strut, regarding it as you would a bar of gold. 'Oh, the deceit of the girl!' he shouted. 'She has set light to my furniture!'

Betsy, struggling to free herself from the shawls that swaddled her, stared at him, terrified.

'I'll pay for the chair,' I said quickly.

'Oh, yes, you will pay for it. Indeed you will!' He crossed to the small window, opened the shutters and leaned out. 'You, boy!' he shouted down. He pulled a coin from his pocket and threw it so that I heard it strike the cobbles. 'Here's a penny. Go for a constable, will you?'

'Is it a fire, sir?' I heard the boy call back.

'Not a fire, a thief! Arson! A malicious destroyer of furniture! Find a constable or go and ask the magistrate to send a Runner! Quick as you like.'

I heard the boy shout something in reply and the land-lord gave a satisfied grunt and closed the shutters.

'Very keen on catching criminals, the Runners. A most efficient policing system.'

I began shaking all over. 'Please,' I said. 'I know I shouldn't have . . .'

'Save your pleas for the court,' he said, and so saying he turned on his heel and went out of the room, locking the door behind him.

Chapter Fifteen

I was too angry to cry, too bewildered, too frightened – and too worried about Betsy. I took her on my knee and tried to comfort and reassure her, but even at five years old she could tell that I was just uttering meaningless words and it was *not* going to be all right. The awfulness had begun the moment we'd arrived in London and it had got steadily worse. I was too scared to think of what might happen to us now.

Mr Burroughs returned with two men: two officious, stout men in navy serge suits who came pounding up the stairs and, on the door being unlocked, came one each side of where I was sitting on the bed, took Betsy away from me and pulled me to my feet. I would have liked to have been brave in front of Betsy but I could not manage it, and began to weep.

'This is the wicked girl, is it, sir?' the first Runner asked the landlord.

'I am not wicked at all!' I cried, and I struggled with them and kicked out at their shins. I know now this was the worst thing I could have done, for if I had acted meek and repentant it would have gone better with me and they would not have been so rough.

'Why, I have never had anyone more wicked under my roof!' Mr Burroughs said. 'Burning my furniture . . . stealing my chickens –'

'Chickens!' I cried, stopping my struggles. 'What would I be wanting with chickens? I haven't even seen any chickens.'

'But you admit to burning furniture?' asked the second Runner.

'I burned a rickety old chair,' I said. 'It could have only been worth a penny or two.'

'She wantonly destroyed good furniture,' said the landlord. 'She came to my house and set fire to my things! That's arson.'

'Is this true?' asked the first Runner.

''Twas only one thing that I burned, and that just because it was fierce cold in the room and the child was not well –'

'I had five chickens when she arrived – now they're nowhere to be seen,' Mr Burroughs interrupted. 'I do b'lieve she's taken them up and sold them!'

'I have not!' I cried. 'There are no chickens and never have been!'

'But, anyway, arson alone is surely a hanging offence,' added the landlord.

I was terrified by this last remark and hoped that Betsy wouldn't understand what it meant. 'I burned a small, old chair for firewood!' I protested, as images of the scaffold rose up before me. In my mind's eye I saw myself kneeling to take a last blessing from a cleric, having a hood fitted, the noose being placed over my head . . .

The first man nodded towards Betsy. 'Is this your own child?'

I shook my head. 'She is my friend's sister.'

'Then why is she with you?'

'Have you kidnapped her to use for begging?' the other wanted to know. 'If you have, it would be as well to confess it now.'

'*Kidnapped?*' I began incredulously.

The landlord made a gesture with his hands, as if to say he'd heard quite enough. 'Just take her away! We are not able to sleep easy in our beds with such wickedness in the house.'

'Do you admit that you burned furniture?' the first Runner asked.

'*Valuable* furniture,' put in Mr Burroughs.

I nodded. There was not much else I could do, seeing as the charred remains of the chair were still smouldering on the fire.

'She is guilty as charged; a wicked and wayward girl who has no place in an honest and God-fearing house.'

Suddenly, realising that the Runners' grip on me had loosened a little while they'd been speaking, I slipped and wriggled out of their grasp and made a dash for the door. I had only reached the top of the stairs, however, when Betsy gave a piercing scream and I stopped in my tracks. How could I go? How could I even think of running away and leaving her?

'You were going without me!' she wailed as the Runners took hold of me once more.

'Of course I wasn't.'

'You were! You were!'

'I was going to escape, then come back and get you later,' I said, already deeply ashamed of myself.

'Take up your possessions,' the first Runner instructed. 'We are going to the courthouse so you can be formally charged.'

'With arson, that will be,' the landlord said, giving a nod and a malicious smile. 'As I said before, a hanging offence.'

Betsy looked at me. 'What does *that* mean?'

I didn't reply, but the landlord – that evil man – replied for me, by putting his hands around his neck and, pulling a grotesque face, pretending to choke himself. Betsy shrank back from him in terror.

'Bring your things and come with us,' said the first Runner.

Turning my back and weeping heartily, I prepared to leave. Packing did not take more than a few seconds, for we had only Betsy's cloth bag and her corn dollies to think about; we were wearing everything else.

We were bundled downstairs, forced out of the house and pushed and pulled through the lanes with the landlord coming up behind. I would have gone quietly so as not to draw attention to ourselves, but Betsy – who was back in full voice – shrieked and struggled with each step she took, so that passers-by turned to stare and even crossed the street to get a better look at whoever-it-was being carted off to Bow Street. Not everyone was on the side of law and order by any means, however, for several women patted Betsy's head and murmured, 'Shame on you' to our captors, and one old man gave me two apples, saying, 'Poor child' with the utmost pity.

The way to the magistrates' court was, unfortunately, past Mr Holloway's dairy, and seeing that he was standing outside, I lifted my shawl and swathed it around my face in the hope that he wouldn't recognise me. It didn't work, though, because he came to ask the Runners what I had been involved in.

The landlord spoke first, butting in rudely to say, 'By speaking to this drab you address an arsonist and a thief. This wicked creature has set fire to my home and stolen my chickens!'

'Indeed?' Mr Holloway said. 'I'm most surprised to hear it.'

'You know I wouldn't do such a thing!' I said to Mr Holloway.

'Don't be deceived by her innocent looks,' the landlord returned. 'She's wicked through and through.'

'Mr Holloway!' I said quickly. 'I'm very sorry about your cows. Betsy was ill and I couldn't leave her.'

'Ah. I thought it might be something of that nature,' he replied, and to my astonishment he pressed two shillings into my hand and said to the Runners that I had been a good and hard-working girl and that he would give me a character reference if it was needed. I was quite overcome at this and would have liked to thank him properly, but there was no time for such a civility before the Runners had hold of me again and I was being marched along with Betsy sobbing and clinging to my skirts.

The next few hours passed in a blur. I just could not believe what was happening to me – to us – on account of such a seemingly small offence. I knew I'd done wrong in breaking up the chair and burning it, but to say that I had committed arson! Surely the magistrate, when I told him about Betsy being ill and the necessity of getting her warm, would make allowances for us? And as for the chickens – well, that was probably some underhand trick played by Mr Burroughs to try and obtain money from the courts. As far as I knew there wasn't even a yard in the lodging house for any chickens to run about in.

We spent several hours waiting in a tiny, windowless box room in the magistrates' court in Bow Street. I was left alone with my thoughts at this time (and you can imagine that they were very dark ones) because the two Runners had been sent to apprehend other criminals and the beast of a landlord had gone away. Betsy fell asleep, and I was pleased about this for it meant I didn't have to keep up the pretence that everything was going to be all right.

At some stage a man wearing a black gown and grey powdered wig came in to say that the charge against me was too serious to be heard by the magistrates and would need the deliberations of a judge and jury.

'Your offence, if deemed to be arson, may be a capital one,' he said. 'Do you understand what that means?'

I nodded, terrified.

'Although 'tis unlikely you will suffer the noose,' he added as an afterthought. A rush of relief ran through my body, but this didn't last for long, for he went on, 'Depending on who the presiding judge is, your offence will probably be commuted to a spell in a pillory or a number of lashes.'

I began to shake, for either punishment sounded terrible. To be in a pillory: to have dead dogs and cats and the contents of latrines thrown at my head! Or to be lashed on my bare back in public!

Someone came in with two bowls of gruel and I woke Betsy so that she could drink hers. It was so thin it could not have had much goodness in it, but at least it was hot. After what seemed like another long time we were taken out into a yard and I had shackles placed on my lower legs. They were made of rusty, stone-cold iron, were tight around my calves and bit into the bones of my ankles. Wearing them was a horror for I felt like a proper and wicked criminal. We were put into a cart with about ten other prisoners, all similarly chained, and I saw that these pitiable wretches were the very poorest of vagabonds and beggars, all smelling foul, some lacking shoes and most wearing repellent, tattered clothing. Seeing this, and knowing that I must look and smell badly, too, I shed a few tears, thinking of how neat and clean I had always kept myself as a milkmaid: my nails scrubbed, my wayward hair coiled and my petticoats snowy white. How quickly my life had changed!

At home I had always enjoyed a ride in a farm cart, jigging along with two dray horses afront, sitting on a hay bale and singing in time to the *clip-clop* of their hooves, but this ride was very different. None of us miserable travellers on the prison cart looked any other in the eye, and folk in the street jeered at us as we went along, catcalling and shouting such things as 'Look! Here comes the King and his court!'. I kept my eyes down the whole time, huddled inside my shawl and spoke to no one.

Betsy was the only one who was not shackled, so sat on my lap during our shameful journey, pressed against me and hardly speaking a word. It would have been possible for me to lift her over the side of the cart so that she could have run away, but I knew this would not have helped her, for there was nowhere safe for her to run to. Having only just begun to recover from the sickness, she would not have been strong enough to survive on her own and would either have died of cold, been picked up by a gang of thieves and trained as a pickpocket, or suffered the perhaps worse fate of being placed in an orphanage. No, I thought, I could not take what would be the easiest path for me, just put her over the side and tell her to run away; I must keep her with me and look after her as well as I could.

After about half an hour's travelling, the cart stopped outside two windowless square blocks, grey-bricked and several storeys high. In front of these was a large open area where, I found out later, public hangings were conducted. We prisoners were driven to a gatehouse in front of one of these blocks, then clambered out of the cart as best we could and stood in a speechless huddle staring around us.

'What is this place?' Betsy asked in a whisper, but I just shook my head, too fraught to reply.

Someone overheard her, though, and a man I later discovered to be a turnkey gave a low, mocking bow. 'Ladies and gentlemen, you are at the doors of London's finest. I bid you welcome to Newgate Prison!'

Chapter Sixteen

I had heard about Newgate Prison, of course; knew of it as the most terrible of all prisons where only the very wickedest of people ended up. The thought that I was actually to be inside it, and with a child dependent on me, felt akin to being in a nightmare.

All natural light had gone by the time we were taken below to the cells, and our way down the long stone corridors was lit by flaming torches on each side of the wall. The light from these didn't carry very far, however, so most of the vast space about us remained in darkness, with who-knew-what lurking in the depths of its murky corners. The stench of filth was indescribable, and a faint, cloying mist hung in the air.

'It smells!' Betsy said, taking hold of her nose.

'It does.' I nodded, breathing in as shallow a way as possible.

'You'll get used to that, dearies,' said the turnkey who was leading us through. 'Soon you won't remember there was any other aroma 'cepting a bad one.'

I did not respond or even glance in his direction, for I had already looked at him once and been horrified to see that he had but one ear, the other having been sliced away, leaving a dreadful, knotted scar. Whether this missing ear was as a result of a brawl, or as punishment for some wicked deed or other, I never found out.

I trudged on with the others, the leg irons gnawing at my skin, and at last came to a large barred area containing perhaps a hundred or so filthy, stinking and unshaven men standing around a brazier, pushing and fighting with each other in order to obtain some warmth from the fire. Here a gate was opened and the men in our little party were left, with one fellow receiving a farewell shove from the earless man which sent him sprawling on to the floor.

We set off again, the turnkey whistling cheerily, and the rest of us – four girls and Betsy – followed in his wake as best we could. Reaching the next large cell, the women's quarters, the gate was unlocked for us and we were told to get in quickly and not hang about or we would miss our roasted swan dinner. Betsy clutched my hand at this and looked up at me hopefully, and I had to tell her that it was a so-called joke on the part of the turnkey, and there were no roasted dinners of swan or anything else to be had in Newgate. One of the girls with us said that we should not expect any food at all that night, for we were too late to receive our daily allowance.

If I'd hoped that the women's accommodation might be somewhat cleaner than the men's then I was sadly disappointed, for it seemed to me even more disgusting – it certainly stank just as badly. There were perhaps sixty or seventy women in the large cell, most of them clustering around the brazier, and I could see immediately that some of them were drunk, for there were two or three fights going on, and one pair was actually on the floor, pulling each other's hair and rolling in and out of the filth, screeching words which I didn't want Betsy to hear.

Two of the girls in our group of new prisoners set off in an almost sprightly manner across the cell to greet acquaintances, but I, knowing no one, shuffled through holding tightly on to Betsy's hand – though whether this was for her benefit or mine, I wasn't sure. We reached the back wall of the vast cell and I stood there feeling strange and giddy, not knowing what to do or how to act. I felt as if I had somehow been removed to a strange place, a country I knew nothing about, where I could not speak the language. It could have been hell, except that hell is hot.

I looked about me. The girls and women were those types who are usually referred to as – I hate to describe my fellow inmates so, but 'twas the truth – the lowest of the low. There was not one clean face to be seen, not a single girl without ratted hair, nor a gown that was not grimy, ragged or had a hemline that was not caked in mud or worse. While most of the women surrounded the brazier, pushing in order to get a view of the fire, rowing, cursing or berating each other, there were many, I was to notice later, who stayed in corners, slumped over and seemingly overwhelmed by sadness, and did not ever speak as much as a word.

'Hello . . .' A girl of about seven had addressed Betsy, who immediately responded. The little girl was sitting on a bench placed along the back wall, beside a woman I presumed to be her mother, who was feeding a baby. Next to her was a middle-aged woman in a dark woollen dress which looked as though it had once been costly. There were two other children playing nearby and I could not help but be pleased to see them, for although it was a lamentable thing that they were there at all, they would surely make Betsy's life a little more endurable.

Betsy said hello back to the girl, and in just a moment the two of them were talking together and she had opened her bag to show off her remaining corn dollies. I looked about me and, too fearful to try and join the large scrum of women around the brazier, moved towards the two women on the bench and asked, very politely, their permission to be seated beside them.

The woman in the woollen dress replied first, saying rather crossly, 'We have paid for this bench, you know!' Her voice, to my surprise, was almost aristocratic; a bit like Lady Cecilia's, and she wore a lopsided wig, curls piled upon curls, a style which had been popular some years back.

I had been about to sit down, but I straightened up again. 'I'm sorry,' I said and, not knowing quite what to do next, bent to look at the grazed and sore patches where the leg irons had rubbed my skin.

'The first thing you want to do is get those fetters off,' the younger woman said. 'Have you any money?'

'A very little.'

She finished feeding, and her baby emerged from under its shawl covering and had its face wiped with a rag. 'For tuppence, one of the turnkeys will knock them off for you,' the young woman said. 'It'll make you feel better, believe me.'

It seemed rude not to take her advice, so I let her direct me to a turnkey who was willing to do this for, as she'd said, the sum of two pennies, and it took but a moment.

'But you may sit with us now for a little while,' the younger woman said, indicating the space on the bench. 'May she not, Mrs Goodwin?'

The other woman shrugged. 'I suppose she may.'

'For our children have already begun to be friends.' The woman smiled at me. 'My name is Martha.'

'Mine is Kitty,' I said. I limped towards them and sat on the edge of their bench, knowing that I was only there under sufferance.

'And this is Mrs Goodwin,' Martha said, and that lady inclined her head towards me like a fine lady in a carriage acknowledging a greeting.

I took some shallow breaths while surveying the scene before me: the glimpsed sight of the glowing brazier, the quarrelling women, the stink, the squalor, the buckets of filth and – most probably – the rats. This was what I'd been brought to. Feeling tears coming, I closed my eyes tightly for a moment and wished with all my might that when I opened them I would be restored to my real life back in the dairy at Bridgeford Hall.

But the screams and the blaspheming and the quarrelling went on and I opened my eyes to find Martha looking at me curiously.

'You have just this moment arrived?' she asked.

I nodded.

'And you have been here before?'

'Never!'

'You were working the streets?'

I felt myself blush, but she spoke in such a matter-of-fact way that I wondered if this was *her* way of life. 'No, not that,' I said. 'My charge, Betsy, was ill and it was so cold in our room that I broke up a chair and used it for firewood.'

'Ah.' She smiled at me sympathetically. 'You were unlucky to get caught.'

'And the landlord said I stole his chickens, too – though I certainly didn't!'

'That will be dismissed as being impossible to prove. But how much was the chair worth?'

'Just a few pennies.'

'Then you will be all right. 'Tis only when you dispose of something worth more than eleven shillings that they deem it a capital offence, you know.'

'But he has said it was worth more. And they have used the word *arson*.'

'Oh, that's much more serious!' said Mrs Goodwin, who had been listening. Her hair wobbled furiously. 'Sometimes, if they want to make an example of you, they give a fearful sentence for arson.'

'They will want to know if your crime was malicious, or if you were just seeking to warm yourself,' Martha said. 'They will also examine your character and try to discover if you have ever been in prison before.'

'I never have!'

'Then I'm sure you'll be all right,' Martha said reassuringly.

Realising that she must have had some previous experience with the law, I asked nervously if she knew what my sentence might be.

Martha checked her baby, who was asleep, then appealed to the aristocratic lady. 'Mrs Goodwin, will Kitty get ten strokes of the lash for a first offence, do you think? Or be pilloried?'

Ten strokes of the lash! Wondering if I would be able to stand it, I asked, 'Would that be better or worse than the pillory?'

'The pillory and the stocks are both shocking, my dear,' Mrs Goodwin said. 'Spending a day and night with your feet or your hands locked in a wooden case whilst at the mercy of others is well-nigh intolerable, especially if the crowd takes against you.' I nodded, thinking of the unfortunate felons we'd seen at Charing Cross the day we'd arrived. 'Ten strokes on your bare back is perhaps the lighter sentence and might be expected for a first offence. And if you bribe the prison officer the lash will not fall on you as harshly as it might.'

I thought about this: ten lashes, and then I would be on my way. That was a better punishment, surely, than being locked into the stocks or pillory? But *ten lashes . . .*

Martha touched my arm. 'I can see how your mind is going, but you won't be able to choose, you know. It'll be up to the judge.'

'Of course,' I said. I hesitated, wondering whether to be so bold, then, Mrs Goodwin appearing to have gone to sleep, asked why Martha was in there.

'This time I am in for theft,' she answered. 'My daughter – Robyn, there – and I were down to our last crust and I went into the draper's and stole a skein of knitting wool, just a trifling thing, which I exchanged for a pie. The draper came after me, but we had eaten the pie before he caught us, so there was no evidence. Now they are trying to find the draper, but he has run off with his master's wife and is not to be found. In the meantime, I have to spend my days here. I have been imprisoned before – about once a year they take me in for some petty thing.'

'But you have a baby . . .'

'I have.' She looked down at the little raggedy bundle. 'And glad I am to have her, for I would have been transported to Australia last month had I not been on the verge of giving birth. Now I hope for a lesser punishment: that I may be sent into a workhouse with my two girls.'

I knew a woman could avoid certain sentences if she could prove she was with child, but was surprised that Martha was content to be sent to a workhouse. I'd never heard of the sentence of transportation, however, and had to ask where Australia was.

She shrugged. 'I hardly know. Just that 'tis a land beyond the seas.'

'Beyond the seas?' I repeated wonderingly. How could that be? Beyond there was . . . nothing, surely? 'But why would anyone be sent to such a place?'

Martha shrugged once more. 'All I know is that you travel to Australia in a big ship and it takes more than a year. I've heard that there are sea monsters on the way – and when you arrive, wild men who will eat you. If they try to send me there again, I will certainly refuse to go!'

'I don't blame you!' I said, in my head weighing up which was preferable: the stocks, the lash, or being sent to this Australia. I looked about me fearfully. 'It is most terrible in here, yet you seem resigned to it. Whatever causes you to return to such a place?'

'What else can a poor girl do? In London it's steal or starve.'

'Can you never find any honest work?'

'Sometimes, in the summer, I can work a few hours on a market stall, and then I eke out what I earn for as long as possible and keep out of trouble. In the winter, though, if I did not pass the odd dud coin or steal sheets off a washing line, we'd go hungry.'

'And does Robyn always come in here with you?'

She nodded. 'I have no one to leave her with, and 'twould break my heart to have her taken away from me.' She gestured towards Betsy. 'But you were unlucky to bear a child so young.'

'Oh, Betsy is not mine!' I said immediately.

She smiled. 'You don't have to make up stories for such as me,' she said. She indicated the baby. 'This little one here, I could not say for sure who her father is.'

I had, I realised, led a very sheltered life before coming to London, and I tried not to look shocked. 'She is a very pretty baby,' I said, although I could not really tell, the baby being too well swaddled to see. 'What's her name?'

'I haven't decided on that yet,' Martha said. 'I am waiting to see what name she suits when she grows a little. So, your child, Betsy . . .'

'No,' I said, 'she is really not mine. She is the sister of a friend – the friend I came to London to find.'

'If she is not yours, why not ask an orphanage to take her in?'

I shivered. 'I could not. I have heard them to be horrid places.'

'*This* is a horrid place!'

'It is,' I agreed readily, 'but at least she has me.' I rubbed my cold arms to try and warm them, wanting to change the subject, for thinking of just why Betsy was here was making me feel uncomfortable. ''Tis monstrous cold!'

'But you wouldn't want to be here when 'tis hot, either – when fever spreads through the wards and people lie half-dead across the floor, groaning and vomiting by turn. Why, they die so fast that the other prisoners have to be employed as gravediggers to help bury them.'

I shuddered.

'But where do you come from?' Martha asked. 'Your accent tells me you are not from round these parts.'

'I come from Devonshire, where I was a dairymaid on a farm,' I said. And as I spoke that past life of mine seemed so idyllic, so sweetly pastoral – and such a contrast from what was around me – that I began weeping.

Martha patted my shoulder, but after a while said gently, 'It will do you no good at all to weep, Kitty. You'd be better occupied finding out when your case is to be heard and deciding what you'll say in your defence.'

After a moment I sighed, dried my eyes as best I could on a corner of my sleeve and asked what I should do.

'You must give the turnkey a penny and ask to see the guv'nor, who's a fair man who can be bribed to do most anything for a pipe of baccy. Say you've a young child with you and you want to know how quickly your case can be heard.'

'Shall I go to see him now?'

'Not now,' Martha said. 'The brazier is being damped down and we must take our rest.'

'Where must we go for that?' I asked, picturing some sort of dormitory. Mrs Goodwin woke up with a start and Martha looked at me curiously.

'Why, nowhere at all,' said Martha.

'But where are our mattresses?'

Mrs Goodwin gave a sudden shout of laughter. 'Mattresses!' she exclaimed. 'Bless the young girl!'

'It's a quaint notion,' Martha said, smiling.

I looked around. 'Is there not even any straw for us?'

'Not so much as a wisp!' said Mrs Goodwin.

And so, after using the bucket in the corner, I spread my skirts on the floor, cuddled Betsy to me and prepared for my first night within the walls of Newgate Prison.

Chapter Seventeen

I did not sleep – of course not. The wailing, screaming, raucous singing and noisy arguments amongst the women went on and on throughout the night by the light of a flickering candle, so much so that I began to think that I had been consigned to a madhouse. It seemed that the women not only hated the prison, but hated each other, and many seemed always drunk, for those who could afford liquor were able to get a plentiful supply of it from the taproom. Indeed, I soon realised that if you had money you could get a plentiful supply of just about anything from the turnkeys, who derived most of their income in this way. Lying sleepless on the stone-cold ground I saw, too, both men and women slipping in and out of the ward gates, and discovered later from Martha that women who were willing to either visit the men's quarters, or entertain a man in theirs, were well paid for it. Some women were even willing to do it for nothing in the hope of getting pregnant, for then they could plead their bellies and perhaps receive a lighter sentence.

It cost me tuppence to see the governor, and, although Martha offered to keep an eye on Betsy, I thought it best to take her with me. Martha seemed very nice – at least, for someone who was frequently in gaol – but as I had learned, I should trust no one. For all I knew there might be a thriving trade in child slavery in the gaol; there was certainly every other kind of depravity.

I had One-ear as my guide to the governor's office and, though he was not very attractive to look at, he maintained a flow of interesting information about the prison and those who dwelt within it. Thus I discovered that there were several different areas within the gaol itself: one side containing those who, like me, could not afford to pay for their upkeep, which was known as the Commons' Side. Another area, the Press Yard, contained those people who were notable or titled, while those who were rich had the distinction of residing on what they called the Master's Side, which meant they were under the direct supervision of the governor and, as long as they could pay for it, could appeal to him for any little trifle they fancied.

'They has the best of everything,' One-ear told me. 'They sends out for food, they has proper beds – four-posters, some of 'em – and clean linens afore they needs 'em. They has parties and folks in to visit when they please. It's a reg'lar home from home. Some keep horses in the stables and come and go as they like.'

I stared at him in surprise.

'And the gentlemen who don't have their wives with 'em always has a steady stream of lady visitors. But I don't mean *ladies*, if you get my meaning.'

He sniggered at this but I did not respond.

'There's a highwayman who comes in reg'lar and uses the gaol as his London residence. Plans his next robberies here, he does.'

'But doesn't he ever get caught and sentenced?'

'Certainly he does,' One-ear said, sounding shocked. 'In he comes, and then he bribes or breaks his way out again, does another crime and comes back. It's like he's on a length o' string!'

The stench got momentarily worse when we passed across what One-ear called a stream but actually was an open sewer into which the inmates could empty their buckets.

Betsy was both fascinated and appalled by the sight of this putrid and nauseating mess flowing sluggishly across our path. 'What's all *that*?' she asked, staring down and holding her nose.

'What do you think?' I said, grabbing hold of her hand to pull her along. 'Come along quickly now. We don't want to get left behind.'

'There's the kitchen,' said One-ear, pointing down a corridor. 'It's there that they cooks all them luvverly foodstuffs you're going to have while you're staying with us.'

Betsy looked at me and I shook my head to say that no, they were not going to be lovely. Despite missing our bread allowance yesterday, neither of us was hungry, for I had discovered that having a loathsome stench permanently in your nostrils quite took your appetite away, although both Martha and Mrs Goodwin assured me that this would pass.

One-ear paused and nodded to a row of stone steps going downwards. 'Down them stairs are the condemned cells.'

I stared down the cold stone passage and shivered.

'They're putting up the viewing stands in the square right now. Three poor blighters – two women coiners and one footpad – gettin' ready to do the Newgate jig!'

'What's the Newgate jig? Is it a special dance?' Betsy asked, then luckily noticed two rats slinking around a corner and went down on all fours in order to see them better.

'What's a coiner?' I asked One-ear, for I had never heard this term before.

'Oh, 'tis a very popular crime in Newgate. The felons take a gold coin, see, and scrape a little from all around the edge of it. Then they pass off the coin as whole, and sell the gold dust to a jeweller.'

'That is a capital crime?'

'Certainly it is,' he said stoutly. 'It bears the King's

head and whether he is a mad King or no, 'tis classed as a crime against him and therefore treason.'

The governor's office was a surprise. Betsy and I followed One-ear up a flight of stone steps, through a heavy door and found ourselves in a well-dressed room, both light and bright with paintings, framed certificates and polished brass lamps. With its green-painted shutters and heavy mahogany desk it looked, to me, very much like the estate manager's office at Bridgeford Hall. The governor, Mr Hallet, was also a surprise, for whereas the turnkeys all seemed to be thin and weaselly, their faces dull through lack of sunlight, Mr Hallet was rotund and florid-faced, his demeanour suggesting good living – and much of it. I later found out that the post of governor was one that could be bought by the highest bidder and could be the means of making one's fortune; it had little to do with whether or not a man was suitable for the position.

I curtseyed, then sat Betsy on a chair at the back of the room and told her not to move or speak, for I had to talk to someone who was very important.

The turnkey announced, 'Kitty Grey,' and left the room. I curtseyed again, murmured good morning and Mr Hallet looked up at me.

He took a book from a drawer. 'Kitty Grey,' he said. 'Are you a new prisoner?'

I nodded. 'Yes, sir. I came in yesterday.'

'He leafed through the book and must have found my name. 'Arson, is it?'

'Please, sir, 'twas not arson. I merely burned a few sticks in the grate to keep myself and the child warm.'

'And the chickens? Roasted them on the fire, did you?'

'I never saw any chickens. I wouldn't know what to do with chickens,' I said earnestly. 'I only burned –'

'Keep your pleas for the court,' he said. He peered at Betsy. 'How old is your child?'

'She is not my child, sir.'

'Not yours? Then what is she doing here?' he asked. 'Have you kidnapped her?'

'Indeed I have not! I brought her to London so that we could find her brother, for she has no other close relatives.'

'Then she has no business being here and taking up valuable space. We already have three times the number here that we should have. Why, if everyone brought in children from the streets there would be no room for prisoners.'

I was completely taken aback. 'Then . . .'

'Then she must go to an orphanage.'

I heard a little squeal from Betsy. 'I don't . . .' she began, and then came a muffled sob.

I thought quickly. 'Sir, I must throw myself on your mercy,' I said. 'I confess she *is* my child. I didn't want to say so, for I thought it would go against me.'

He looked at me sternly. 'And where is your husband?'

'I have no husband. She was . . . was born out of wedlock.'

'Yes, I thought that would be the case,' he said drily.

'I said what I did about her because . . . because I did not want to gain a certain reputation.'

'In here, everyone has a reputation.'

'So may she stay with me? If it pleases you, sir,' I added humbly.

'She may stay for the present, until the court decides what your sentence should be.' He ran his fingers down a line of figures. 'Ah, I see someone, a Mr Holloway, has offered to pay your garnish.'

I must have looked mystified at this because he added, 'Mr Holloway, a cow-keeper, has offered to pay the daily charge for your bread and meat. Is he the father of this child?'

I felt myself go pink with embarrassment. 'No, sir, he is not. I have only known him a matter of days.'

'Indeed?' It was all too plain what he was thinking. 'What a kind gentleman he must be then, because for some reason of his own he wishes to help you.'

'Then I am very grateful to him,' I said, and indeed I was, for it had not occurred to me I would have had to pay for my food. 'But can you tell me when my case is likely to be heard, sir?'

'With luck, within a week,' he said, 'for they are trying to clear all straightforward cases by Christmas and allow us a little breathing space in the gaol.'

I hesitated. 'And have you any idea what my sentence might be?'

But as I had nowhere near enough money to admit

me to the Master's Side and so help line his pockets, he seemed to have lost interest. He closed the accounts book and poured himself a drink from a glass decanter. 'It depends whether you catch the judge before dinner or after it. And if someone has moistened the jury's throats with a swig or two of gin. But arson is bad. Arson could go either way.'

'It really was not arson, sir.'

'It's not me you need to convince, girl!' he retorted, then nodded towards the door. I curtseyed deeply, picked up Betsy and went out.

'You said you borned me, didn't you?' Betsy asked, whispering in my ear.

'I did.'

'So shall I call you Mummy now?'

'If you want to,' I said, sighing, and then looked at her poor little grubby face and tried to smile. 'Of course you can, if you'd like to.'

'But even if you are my mummy, we'll still look for Will, won't we?'

'Of course.' I nodded, but my heart wasn't in it. I had realised by then that it would be near impossible to find Will in London.

One-ear was waiting outside and escorted me back a different way through the tunnels and corridors so that I had several more glimpses of the fine life that could be led in gaol if you were rich: I saw a cell which was more like a shop and sold all manner of things, a busy tavern, a private dining room and a laundry room where a maidservant sat sewing. I also glimpsed, through a window, the scaffold being erected for the following day's hangings, and gave more than one thought to the sorry creatures who were to receive this punishment.

Chapter Eighteen

❀

The prison population went into a frenzy about the hangings. These were scheduled for eight o'clock in the morning, and by four o'clock, when it was still dark as fury outside, all of the gaol inmates were awake and banging on the floor or at the metal bars of the cells with tin cups, spoons or any other implements they could find.

There was a small barred window high up in the wall where the scaffold could be glimpsed in the square outside, and here stands had been erected with seats at one shilling in order that the wealthy might see the better. About six o'clock, as it grew lighter, one tall young woman amongst us climbed on another's shoulders to report what was happening.

'Scores of people are coming every minute,' she said excitedly. 'Men, women and children, peddlers, hot-piemen, sellers of baked chestnuts and men on horseback. You should just see them!'

As time went on and it grew closer to eight o'clock, other women took her place and continued the commentary in turn. Even if you didn't want to hear it, you could do little to escape, for each sentence uttered by the seeing-woman was repeated by others and the words spread outwards across the cell like ripples on a pond.

'Someone's family have arrived . . . there is a man weeping piteously.'

'A woman is prostrate with grief at the foot of the scaffold.'

'I see a thief picking the pocket of a fellow in a greatcoat!'

'Someone is shouting that a reprieve will come from the King.'

I found it hard to know what to say to Betsy about what was going on, for how could I explain the fearsome concept of death? I did not want her to think, either – oh, let it not be true! – that such a punishment might befall me. I kept her close by my side, therefore, and just told her that there was a big meeting outside and some people were very cross about it, and some very excited. Mrs Goodwin said that I should tell her the truth; that knowing what happened to thieves and highwaymen might keep her on the path of righteousness in later life, but I did not agree as I deemed her far too young.

At ten minutes to eight there was a poignant sigh from the crowd outside which seemed to seep through the very walls of the gaol and settle over us. We all looked around at each other uneasily.

'One of the women has appeared and it has quieted the crowd,' said the girl now viewing the scene. 'I believe 'tis Eliza Branning.'

'What does she have on?' several voices asked eagerly.

'A lilac bonnet and her hair is up. She is wearing a pretty muslin gown with white lace.'

There was another sigh, from the women inside this time, for we were all wearing the very worst and filthiest attire and most of us would have given a great deal to be dressed in a muslin gown and lilac bonnet. Looking around, I realised that most of the women were wearing oversized men's clothes: heavy jackets and waistcoats, for, of course, these were warmer and probably proved more durable inside a prison.

'And what is happening now?' came the cry from around me.

'The cleric has arrived and is speaking to Eliza. She is kneeling to pray . . . Ah, now she is standing, removing the bonnet and passing it to someone in the crowd. The hangman is fitting a hood over her head.'

'They always dress up nicely to be hanged,' Martha whispered in my ear.

'But what if they have no good clothes to wear?'

'Then someone will lend them something suitable – I believe the governor has a trunk of such things. Men often dress as bridegrooms.'

I asked why.

'They want to be looking their best in case a tavern buys their outfit and exhibits it on a replica of them afterwards,' she explained. 'They do this if the felon is a famous highwayman or someone else loved by the people.'

I marvelled very much at this.

'But the last hanging here was most distressing, for 'twas of a woman who mounted the scaffold still feeding her baby,' Martha said. 'They had to take it out of her arms to put the noose around her neck.'

'Tell me no more!' I begged, and turned away.

I had, I realised, changed my opinion about those who were commonly called thieves, for I knew now that for many of them taking a loaf from a market stall was the only way they could ensure their children received any nourishment. Many so-called paupers could only receive Poor Relief if it was claimed within the parish they had been born in, so hardly any of that great number who came to London to find work received aid.

I took Betsy and her friend Robyn over to the furthest corner of the cell, and here we invented a game which involved throwing a corn dolly into a circle we had made out of gravel. Thus we managed to occupy ourselves through the banging and stamping and cries of 'Shame!' which accompanied the deaths of the three poor souls. No reprieves arrived for them, which I thought a great pity.

Following the hangings and the raising of the black flag outside, it took a day or so for the gaol to simmer down. I went on as before, trying not to antagonise anyone (for some of the women there would attack another for an imagined slight or sideways glance), endeavouring to keep Betsy amused and taking our incarceration minute by minute. I tried not to think too much about what might lay ahead.

Because kindly Mr Holloway (I had, of course, completely reversed my previous opinion of him) was paying one shilling a day to the governor's office I was able to have a few little luxuries in gaol. I smile at calling them such, for they were only what everyone down to the lowliest bootboy had as a matter of course in Bridgeford Hall: a thin, straw mattress to sleep on, milk to drink and a little cooked meat at dinner time. I had also obtained a blanket which, though grubby and worn, kept off the draught from the barred window above us and, with this blanket over and the straw mattress under, I sometimes managed to get a few hours' uninterrupted sleep at night.

Women were allowed outside for half an hour a day to exercise, but few took up this privilege, for there was a men's ward next to our walking area and, by climbing up their wall, they could see us and subject us to any amount of abuse and foul language, spitting and catcalling. Besides, it was bitterly cold outside now and, so a popular story had it, a girl had walked around the perimeter of the wall but twice and got frostbite, following which she lost all her fingers. When I heard that I spread my hands and looked at them hard: at the grime now etching the lines on my palms, and the dirt under my nails. My hands had once been pale and soft, smooth as a lady's hands because of the buttermilk rubbed into them, but now they were as filthy and stained as those of a street child. At least I had the use of them, though; if I lost them to frostbite I'd never be able to milk a cow again! This thought brought tears to my eyes (indeed, they were never far away) and I quickly sought out Betsy and occupied myself teaching her and Robyn their letters, writing in the dust on the floor with a stick.

About ten days after I'd arrived, the women in my ward were greatly cheered to have a visit from a wealthy society lady by the name of Mrs Elizabeth Fry. She arrived on a Wednesday afternoon and at first we thought she was one of the usual visitors who were allowed in twice a week for the sport of it. They would arrive with a party of friends and walk about with a kerchief to their noses, exclaiming at the smell and conditions and looking at us with horror, then go home to their elegant houses and forget about us. She was not of this ilk, however.

Betsy met her first. She was playing with Robyn and some other children – there were nine altogether in our ward – when she ran over to tell me that a grand lady had arrived on her own.

'A very grand lady!' she reported. 'The turnkey didn't want her to come in without an escort because he said that the women would set about her and steal her fine things.'

'Did he indeed?'

'He wanted her to take off her jewellery and watch at the gate, but she wouldn't.'

'And then what?'

'Now she is talking to the children and admiring the babies.'

'Then go back quickly in case she is giving something away!' I said, for occasionally one of the society ladies who visited would give the children a sweetmeat or piece of gingerbread.

This lady stayed on, talking earnestly to several of the girls, and after a short while curiosity got the better of us and Martha and I went over to her. She spoke to us very gently and politely (which we were not at all used to in there), asking us about our backgrounds and wanting to know how we came to be in the gaol, which she called an abode of misery and despair.

'But I am shocked to see many of you wearing men's clothes,' she said when we had briefly told her our stories. 'It looks very brutal and indelicate and I fear may make a woman forget the gentler part of her nature.'

'These clothes are all we have, madam,' several of us replied.

'Then I shall send you in some gowns that I've been collecting,' she said. There was a stir of excitement at this. 'And I will take down the ages of the children so that they may have clean clothing, too.'

We all curtseyed our thanks, and I think each one of us was trying to outdo the other in gentility, so that Mrs Fry might remember us in particular.

'Is there anything else you wish for?' she asked.

One woman spoke of the hatefulness of having nowhere to wash ourselves, another said they would like to eat meat a little more often, and I ventured to say that if something could be supplied for the children to play with – even just a ball or some chalks – then that would give them something to amuse themselves with through the long days.

Mrs Fry smiled at me. 'You have a child here?'

I nodded and pointed to Betsy, doing so without any embarrassment, for I'd realised that no one else there cared a ha'penny button whether she was my own child or not.

'As a matter of fact, I am thinking of starting a little school,' Mrs Fry said. 'I have a friend who's a governess and she is willing to come in three times a week and give lessons to the children. This will, perhaps, enable them to have a better start in life.'

We all expressed our pleasure at this, and some of the other women asked if they could also attend the classes, as they could neither read nor write and wanted to learn.

The great lady seemed pleased. 'I am gratified by your response,' she said in her gentle voice. 'Once the classes for children are established, I intend to start Bible-reading classes and teach needlework, for I am of the opinion that habits of order, industry and sobriety will improve things for everyone.'

'But they'll surely never permit classes,' said Mrs Goodwin, who by then had also joined us.

'I think they will,' Mrs Fry said with a smile. She was very beautifully dressed with a fur muff and matching bonnet, and she rose and adjusted this latter as she spoke. 'It has always seemed to me that if people are treated like animals then they will behave like animals, but if they are permitted to go about their lives with dignity, then a great good will come of it.'

So saying, she touched the hands of those gathered about her (not even looking at the grime upon them!) and called a turnkey to unlock the gate, leaving us to marvel at the promises she'd made and the thought that someone seemed to care about our welfare. Only a hardened few said that nothing would come of it, that do-gooders had visited before and made promises about food, mattresses and the like which had never been kept.

In the days following we talked of little else but the promised clothes. They had still not arrived, however, when I received a message to say that my trial was to take place the next morning, and would be the tenth to be heard that day. Martha was very cast down by this news; firstly at the thought of Betsy and me going from the gaol (for Betsy and Robyn had become the best of friends) and also because she herself had been held in prison for several months and, as she frequently said, her newborn babe had never yet breathed the fresh air of freedom. The several witnesses to her crime having disappeared, she was hoping that a prison official would take up her case and petition for her release.

Mrs Goodwin took it upon herself to advise me on my court appearance. 'You must look as meek and demure as possible,' she said. 'Pay particular attention to the judge. Be sure to call him "Your Honour" and curtsey every time you address him.'

I nodded, already terrified. I was anxious to get my court appearance over with, of course, but the thought of any punishment alarmed me very much. I was not a brave person and the stocks, the pillory, the lash all seemed equally terrible. I was not allowing myself to think, even for one moment, about the ultimate penalty. Surely, if there was any justice in the world, that would not be allowed to happen?

The following morning manacles were put back on my legs and I was chained with about twelve other prisoners, both men and women. Together we shuffled in a line to the Old Bailey, a forbidding building right next to the prison, separated from it by a passageway with high brick walls, where we were to stand trial.

Mrs Goodwin had lent me an extra shawl (her best one, she emphasised, stolen some years ago from an exclusive draper's in Paradise Row) and I had tied it around my head, for the weather was bitterly cold and even the few breaths I took 'twixt gaol and courthouse caught painfully at the back of my throat. I was feeling very down, both because I feared what sort of sentence I would receive, and also because I had spent several distressing moments with Betsy clinging to me, sobbing and asking me not to go. I had promised her that I would return as soon as I could, and in the meantime entrusted her to Martha's care.

There was a little crowd waiting outside the Old Bailey to watch the arrival of the day's prisoners, and I believe it was then, blinking around me in the daylight, that I felt at my very worst and most degraded. I looked, I knew, like a common beggar, for I was dressed in ill-matched bits and pieces, with filthy, knotted hair and a grimy face, and did not need the little group of society people standing there in their furs and velvets to make me feel any worse.

We prisoners entered a type of waiting room, which turned out to be just below the court itself, and then came a long wait during which, being occupied by our own thoughts, none of us spoke a word to each other (saving a madman with us who said, over and over again, 'Jack's a pretty boy!' in the manner of a parrot). One by one, each member of our party had their shackles knocked off and went up the wooden ladder into the court, and – from listening hard – I heard each of them addressed in a commanding voice by someone I took to be the judge. Twice I heard laughter: once when the madman had to answer a charge of burglary and would say no more than his parrot phrase, and once when a girl who had been chained next to me, by the name of Sarah, was accused of being a pickpocket, and admitted that she had been arrested twenty-six times before. I did not hear all the sentences given, only that Sarah was to be transported for twenty years, one man was to be branded, and the madman told he would be sent to Bethlem Royal Hospital for the rest of his life.

It was with great trepidation that I finally heard my name called. My shackles were removed and I was prodded up the ladder. Trembling, holding on to a rail to steady myself, I found I was standing in a wooden box affair within a vast church-like space. Alongside were polished wooden benches holding legal men in black and, on the first floor, a public gallery containing the type of befurred members of society who had gathered to stare at us outside. The fug of tobacco hung in the air and there were bowls of vinegar placed about, which (Mrs Goodwin had already told me) were precautions against gaol fever being passed from prison to court.

A dark-gowned clerk of the court told me to remove the scarf from around my head and instructed me to turn in a certain direction. I found out later that this was so that the daylight from a mirrored reflector could fall on my face and allow the court to see my expression, thus helping them decide whether I was guilty or not.

I realised I was facing the judge, a burly figure in robes and a lavish wig, and, remembering Mrs Goodwin's words, I sank into a deep curtsey.

A different clerk asked my name and then my address and, not knowing what to say, I answered that I lived in Newgate Prison. This provoked some laughter, so I

amended it to Bridgeford Hall, in the village of Bridgeford, Devonshire.

'You are accused of arson,' the clerk said, 'in that you
did feloniously and wickedly set fire to a room in a
lodging house belonging to Daniel Burroughs, Esquire.
How do you plead?'

'Not guilty, Your Honour,' I said.

'And what is your defence?'

'I *did* set fire to an old chair . . .'

There was a murmur in the court.

'. . . but it was only in the fireplace, Your Honour,
whereas *arson* makes it sound as if I had lit up the very
house. I had to light a fire because my child was sick and
very cold and I was frightened for her life.'

'Most people use coal on their fires, not chairs,' the
judge remarked, and there was some laughter at this.

'I did not have the money for coal,' I said clearly. 'I
bought some firewood, but it burned quickly and I
did not dare leave her to go out and buy more.' The
judge did not comment so I added, 'It was a very old
chair, Your Honour – not worth more than a few
coppers.'

'It was a good and sturdy chair!' came an objection
from elsewhere, and I looked to see my enemy, the
horrid Mr Burroughs, standing behind a table on the
courtroom floor.

'If it had been sturdy, Your Honour, then I could not
have broken it up so easily,' I said very politely.

The judge looked down at the papers before him.

'Sturdy or no, you should not have burned it, for it didn't belong to you.' He looked over towards one of the court clerks. 'Is there anything against this girl? Has she any previous convictions?'

'I have found nothing, Your Honour,' said the clerk. 'There was some business about chickens, but it seems that Mr Burroughs cannot prove he ever had any.'

'Anything else?'

'She is unmarried and has a child,' said the clerk, 'so her morality is in doubt.'

The judge studied me. 'You have a child?'

I hesitated, then answered, 'Yes, I have, Your Honour.'

He shook his head. 'You have embarked on a life of vice at a very young age.'

'Indeed! 'Tis a disgusting and immoral state of affairs!' Mr Burroughs barked.

I could feel my face reddening. 'She is . . .' I began, but didn't go on. This wasn't just because I didn't want Betsy to go into an orphanage, but also for more selfish reasons: I'd got used to her being close to me now, my little companion and friend. She was my only link with home – and with Will.

The judge addressed the jury, who were twelve men sitting six by six in the body of the court. One looked asleep, two others were chatting between themselves and one was smoking a pipe. 'This young woman is clearly guilty,' the judge said, 'but whether of arson or the less serious crime of common theft it is for you to decide.'

'May I speak for her character, Your Honour?' came a voice, and I was both pleased and grateful to see Mr Holloway standing on the floor of the court.

'Quickly, then,' said the judge.

'This young person was employed by me for several days as a milkmaid, and was a conscientious and careful worker. I believe she would not have committed this crime if her child had not been sick and she had not been desperate.'

The judge nodded. 'The jury may or may not take this into consideration.'

Mr Holloway continued, 'I think you will find that Mr Burroughs, the landlord, has brought other cases against young girls who have taken rooms in his house. He seems to take against them for little or no reason.'

The judge looked at Mr Holloway sternly. 'It is not Mr Burroughs who is before the court this morning.'

'No. I beg your pardon, Your Honour,' said Mr Holloway humbly. He flashed a glance at me. 'I would just like to say that if the court finds Miss Grey innocent of all the charges, I would be willing to employ her again.'

My heart leapt – only to sink again at the judge's next words. 'The court cannot dismiss the charge, for she has admitted that she took up the chair and burned it. An example must therefore be made of her behaviour.' He gestured towards the jury. 'You may now decide on your verdict.'

The jury stood up and got into a huddle and, it seemed

to me, did not spend more than a moment discussing my case before they all sat down again.

'Do you find Katherine Grey guilty or not guilty of arson?' the judge asked.

Their spokesman stood. 'Not guilty, Your Honour.'

'And what of the charge of theft?'

'Guilty.'

I closed my eyes briefly. When I opened them the judge was regarding me coldly.

'Kitty Grey,' he said, 'our streets and our city must be rid of women such as yourself. You are sentenced to seven years' transportation to Parts Beyond the Seas.' He nodded to one of the clerks. 'See that she is shackled and taken back to gaol. She can leave on the next boat.'

Chapter Nineteen

I was in a daze when I returned to the prison. Betsy was happy to see me back, but after kissing me heartily a few times, returned to play with Robyn. I was glad of this – that she could not properly understand the implications of the sentence that had been handed down to me.

'Seven years Beyond the Seas,' I whispered to Mrs Goodwin and Martha in response to their enquiry. 'Seven years . . .'

Martha gave a little scream and Mrs Goodwin said, 'That means for life, of course. For I've never heard of anyone coming back again. Once you get *beyond* anywhere, how could you return?'

'I would rather be hanged!' Martha said roundly. 'If my sentence turns out to be transportation, then I'll tell them to do away with me instead.'

I looked at her, then pointed first to Robyn, then to the baby at her breast. 'Would you really?'

She went quiet for some time, regarding me glumly. 'Well, maybe not. 'Tis an awful fate, though, to be eaten by cannibals,' she said eventually.

'Tush!' Mrs Goodwin said. 'Why would they send people there to be eaten? If the idea is to kill you as soon as you arrive, then why wouldn't they kill you here and save the expense of a ship?'

We were silent at this.

'I was talking yesterday to one of the turnkeys,' Mrs Goodwin said, 'and he told me that they are preparing a ship which will sail to this land, Australia, with only women aboard.' She turned to me. 'More than likely you will go on this.'

'Only women? To sail the ship?' Martha asked, incredulous. 'The women will be asked to climb the masts and put out the rigging?'

'No, of course not!' said Mrs Goodwin. 'The women will be *cargo*. They're being despatched to settle with male prisoners who've already been deported.'

'Never!' said Martha with another little scream, while I drew in a shocked breath.

'They have men aplenty in the colonies, but need more women there in order that they may raise families and help populate the country,' Mrs Goodwin went on.

I thought about what this might mean. 'Raise families? But do girls get to choose who they'll raise a family with? Can they say no to a man if they wish?'

She shrugged. 'I have no idea whether 'tis a free-for-all

or if the women have any choice in the matter. If the men are allowed to choose anyone they wish, then those women who look healthy and capable of bearing a clutch of children will be chosen first.'

Robyn and Betsy ran up then with some tale or other of a man who had, this morning, got out of the gaol by hiding in an empty beer barrel and going out on a brewery dray.

When they'd gone again Mrs Goodwin continued in her well-modulated voice, 'When a prisoner has served out his sentence in Australia, or at least proved trust-worthy, he is to be given a wife, a plot of land and a chance to make something of himself. 'Tis a tidy plan for the authorities: they make space in our prisons over here, rid the London streets of those with doubtful morals and at the same time help populate the colonies.'

'But to go to such a country!' said Martha. She shuddered. 'And perhaps to become an old man's darling.'

'In my mind, 'tis a deal better than being hanged,' Mrs Goodwin said.

But I felt as Martha did. I did not want to be chosen by just anyone and have to give him a clutch of children. Even when I spoke later to Sarah, the industrious shoplifter who had been sentenced to be transported for twenty years, and she said that perhaps we'd be chosen by young and handsome highwaymen, I found little comfort. I wanted to do my own picking and choosing. Thinking about this long into the night, I found it maddening to realise that, given the choice of anyone in the world, I would still have chosen Will.

I had no knowledge of when we might be moved to the ship but, asking around the women's ward later, discovered several other girls who had already been sentenced to transportation. Seven years was the minimum term, but one girl of no more than twelve years of age had got thirty years in the colonies, and two had got life. As Mrs Goodwin had remarked, however, it surely made little difference whether you were sentenced to two years or two and twenty, for no one knew anyone who had come back. The journey out there would take over a year, people said, and along the way the ship would stop in places that were mighty hot and very strange, with all sorts of gigantic animals and coloured birds, and – stranger still – creatures such as a very small race of people who talked in a language that couldn't be understood by anyone. Sarah said she was excited at the thought of seeing such sights, but I was not and thought that I'd rather have seen one of my precious cows than an ugly creature covered all over in scales.

The day after, Mrs Fry arrived with a consignment of clothing on a little handcart. I was relieved to see her standing at the gate waiting to be admitted, for I'd feared that Betsy and I would be taken away before she came back and be shipped off to Australia in the tattered garments we stood up in. I still did not want to go, of course. I feared the very thought of travelling to the other side of the world, but I certainly did not want to go in rags.

Mrs Fry had managed to accumulate a huge number of gowns, some with matching hats. On us expressing surprise at this, she said that she had been collecting the garments for some time, and mostly they had been donated by wealthy society ladies who had recently changed their style of gowns from the overblown crinoline shape in brocade and rich fabrics to the newly fashionable, and far simpler, empire line. Those who had embraced this fashion with a wardrobe of new clothes had, with a little prompting from Mrs Fry, donated their old garments to needy prisoners. As most were made in heavy fabrics they would be quite warm, although we would not, of course, wear either hoops or layers of petticoats underneath.

Some girls did not want new clothes. Some were past caring about such things, some were half-mad and snarled if you went near them, several were heavily pregnant, others had lost all self-respect and were content to languish and decay in whatever tawdry item they'd happened to be wearing when they'd arrived in Newgate.

I managed to secure a tidy day gown for myself and two smocks for Betsy, while Mrs Goodwin and Martha were also pleased with their gowns – the former especially, as she'd obtained a blue bonnet with three vertical ostrich feathers which she took to wearing on top of her wig. This grand style attracted the attention of the Wednesday visitors, who would listen, enthralled, to her tall tales of a titled husband who'd perished, a great house burned to the ground and costly jewellery lost – and usually give her a silver sixpence by way of compensation.

Mrs Fry had a calm and smiling presence. She called us all 'ladies' and, in front of her, we behaved as if we were. We did not grab at the clothes, or shove each other out of the way to get to the best things, but found ourselves saying politely, 'I think you might find this more suitable . . .', 'This is surely your colour' and 'I believe this may be your size'.

Martha's baby, who had now been named Elizabeth in honour of Mrs Fry, was given several new and unused miniature nightgowns. I did wonder *why* they were unused, but kept this thought to myself.

Some women put on their new garments straight away and paraded up and down as if they were shopping at the Royal Exchange, but as I'd been told that on arriving at the ship we would be allowed to wash ourselves, I'd decided to keep my new gown (grey cotton, with a tucked front and pearl buttons) until then. I wondered how I would keep it safe, but then Mrs Goodwin told me that for a couple of pennies one could buy a wooden crate from the Newgate turnkeys and your things could be stored below ground.

When Mrs Fry had distributed all the clothes and her barrow was empty, I approached her to ask her advice about getting a letter to my family, for I needed to tell them what had happened and inform them where I was bound. By now, I thought, they would probably have reached the conclusion that I'd died. Sometimes, if I was feeling especially morbid, I would picture my dear mother dressed all in black, journeying to London to lay flowers on a pauper's grave, which vision would always reduce me to tears.

'There is a scribe available in the gaol,' Mrs Fry said in answer to my query, 'and for tuppence he will write any letter you wish.' She smiled at me kindly. 'The shock of hearing that you're in prison and about to be transported will be very great, but it will be infinitely preferable to them believing you're dead. Can your parents read?'

'Alas, they cannot,' I said. 'But there is a woman in the next cottage who can read a letter. Do you know what it will cost to post?'

'It will cost you nothing,' said Mrs Fry, 'because the recipient will have to pay on its arrival. Are your family able to do that?'

'I believe so,' I said, but the truth was, I didn't know. It all depended on so many things: whether the summer harvest had been good, if my father had tuppence to spare that week and if they realised that the letter was from me.

I paid a turnkey a penny to ask the scribe to come into the women's quarters, and he appeared the following afternoon with quill, ink and parchment. After a great deal of thought and hesitation on my part, he wrote, under my direction:

Dearest Mother and Father,

I have to tell you the sorrowful news that I am presently in Newgate Prison and about to be transported to Australia. I fear the circumstances which brought this punishment on to my head are too long to tell here, but rest assured that they do not mean that I have done anything wicked or immoral. Please also be advised that I have with me a young child, Betsy Villiers, who, although an orphan, may have other members of her family enquire for her. If they do, please pass on the knowledge that she is safe and well.

To help regain our family's good name, please be kind enough to send word to Bridgeford Hall to tell them that Miss Alice's bag and money were stolen from me the moment I arrived in London. It was this crime which led directly to my downfall.

I will endeavour to tell you of my safe arrival in Australia and let you know how I am faring. In the meantime, please know that I think of you every day, and remain,
Your loving daughter,
Katherine

I did the best I could with the address, stating that they lived near the Bear and Bull Tavern, and paid another ha'penny over the tuppence to have the letter sealed with red wax. It looked very important when it was completed and would probably frighten the life out of them, for I couldn't remember them ever having received a letter before.

I sat down and cried when the letter-writer had gone, for writing to my parents had caused me to realise that I would probably never see them again in this life. I prayed for everything to go smoothly: that the scribe was a man to be trusted, that the post office would put my letter in the right bag, that a highwayman would not snatch it on its way to Devonshire, that the address would be understood and that my father had a spare tuppence in his pocket to pay for its delivery. There were so many reasons why my letter might not be delivered that I just had to trust to luck. And then I cried a little more for, since coming to London, luck had not been a friend to me.

Chapter Twenty

I tried to imagine myself in this new land. We would not be made to wear shackles once we were there, they said, for there was nowhere for us to escape to. If we were too young or too old to be taken as wives, we would work in what they called a factory house (which sounded much like a workhouse), carding wool, picking oakum or doing some other monotonous task. They said the weather was all topsy-turvy: that when it was hot in England, in Australia it would be cold enough to freeze milk.

I tried to imagine the long, long journey, and what it would be like to sail across the sea for days and months and see nothing around but water, and came to the conclusion that I would not be able to bear it. Some people were dreadfully seasick, apparently, and fell over when they tried to walk. Other prisoners caught fevers and died on board, for the conditions down below the decks on some ships were as bad as at Newgate. If you died when the ship was at sea, you would be wrapped in canvas and thrown overboard to be eaten by fish.

It was a week after Mrs Fry's second visit that those of us who had been sentenced to be sent to Parts Beyond the Seas were told to collect our things ready to go to the ship. This sent Martha into a frenzy of sobs which affected both Robyn and Betsy, while I remained relatively calm, for I could not believe I was really going. Why, I hardly believed there *was* such a land across the seas; it seemed as remote as heaven or the kingdom they say is inhabited by faeries. Surely something would happen to prevent my leaving: they would say that my sentence was a mistake, that they knew I had not meant any harm, that I should be spared. Surely Will would gallop up to the ship on a white horse and rescue us!

But nothing of that sort happened and I said my goodbyes to Mrs Goodwin and to Martha – which was especially hard – and waited with Betsy, my wooden crate in my arms, feeling as if I was in a dream.

At the prison gates, the sight of two small children plus eight sobbing girls waiting to have their shackles put on was a very sorry one. It did not help matters, either, when we were given a send-off which was much like that given to those about to be hanged, with the other female inmates rattling the bars, stamping on the ground and shouting protests about us being made to leave our mother country. I noticed that Sarah wasn't amongst our number, and found out later that she was not well enough to travel, being ill with the fever.

As we prisoners came outside to get into the waiting cart, a change came upon us, for the sky was blue and the air fresh and frosty, which suddenly stopped our tears and made us blink like badgers in the sharp sunlight. For a moment I was reminded of my cows when spring arrives and they leave their winter quarters to be turned out into pasture: how they stretch, bellow and kick up their legs with the joy of no longer being confined. There was no joy for us in thinking of what lay ahead, but it was so good to be outside that I closed my eyes, turned my face towards the silvery sun and took in great gulps of fresh air. And when Betsy asked me why all the bells were ringing, I realised that it was not merely because it was Sunday, but Christmas morning.

This tiny moment of elation didn't last, and we were silent as we climbed into the cart. We sat on the floor and huddled together for warmth, for despite the blue sky and sun it was dismally cold. I did not know any of my fellow captors; two of them came from the Master's Side and the others, in all the great press of people, I hadn't really noticed before. In gaol you tended to keep yourself to yourself – and besides, it was difficult to distinguish between us, for with our torn gowns, filthy faces and matted hair we were just a raggle-taggle band of disorderly women. After a while, one of the three burly guards announced that we were heading for a boat waiting at Swan Dock which would take us on to Galleon's Reach, a way down the Thames towards the sea, and that we would be most of the day getting there. At Galleon's Reach waited the ship we would be sailing on, the *Juanita*.

We received this news in silence, for I believe we were all drained and dulled by the enormity of what was happening to us. Betsy fell asleep and I covered her up with a shawl and tucked her tightly against me, but I was too cold to sleep and was seized with a violent shivering. How could this be happening? I thought about those at home and wondered if my letter had reached them, thought about Miss Sophia returning to the hall, and the surprising kindness of Mr Holloway. Mostly I thought about Will; where he could be and what he would say if he knew what was happening to us. Oh, surely the news would cause him a little anguish?

The road beyond the city became worse – potholed and treacherous – and at length we reached a small jetty where a long, low rowing boat was awaiting us. With difficulty, for we were all still in chains, the watermen on it helped us climb aboard. The captain of the vessel came and looked us over, then asked one of our guards if we were likely to cause any trouble.

'Not they!' came the reply. 'They've not the strength to cause a fuss.'

Our boat cast off and, as we continued downriver, the number of ordinary houses decreased and the wharves and warehouses grew more numerous, as did the river traffic. At first it was mostly small rowing boats, ferries, lighters and tugs going backwards and forwards (and you can imagine that I scrutinised the ferries and those who rowed in them most carefully); later we saw tall-masted ships unpacking their cargoes of tea, sugar and coal, oblivious to what day of the year it was. As hard as I looked, though, and as desperately as I prayed, I did not see the one ferryman I sought.

By now we were all too tired, too cold and too miserable to even weep at our fate, but sat on the floor of the boat as if turned to statues. As the city receded and the scene at each side of the river changed from busy wharves to a gloomy wilderness of swamps, mud and desolation, each of us was locked in our own thoughts. When we came upon a great lumpen mass of a ship, without sails or cannon, half-sunk in the river, we looked at it with a little curiosity, but did not comment.

When a second mighty – yet unkempt and uncared-for – ship came into sight, however, half-buried in mud, and someone read out, 'The *Brunswick*', I could not but wonder aloud what it was doing there.

'"Tis a prison ship with well-nigh a hundred men and guards on board,' said one of those who rowed us. 'A *hulk*, they call it. It was towed to its spot and cannot move.'

'But why are they imprisoned so?' one of the girls asked.

'Because the gaols are too full to take 'em,' came the brief answer. 'And out here on the marshes yon prisoners can fight and wrestle and starve and kill each other and few will know or care.'

As we passed the *Brunswick*, our guard told us that the stink from the ship was not to be borne in summer at low tide. 'The hulk just sits there in its own mess until the river comes in and washes everything away,' he explained cheerily. 'But then again, if the men weren't put in there, they'd be in Newgate. 'Tis hard to choose between 'em.'

'Why don't they just swim to shore and escape?' one of our number asked.

'Swim? Wearing leg irons and through such terrain?' the guard replied. 'These marshlands stretch for miles – any creature jumping ship would lose his way and certainly perish amidst mud and quicksand.'

'They do try it occasionally,' another remarked. 'We find their bones washed up on the spring tide.'

We came to yet another stranded ship, deep in silt and decay and hanging with weeds and wet clothing, named the *Unicorn*.

'Aye. Another hulk,' said the guard. 'She was a fine ship once . . . fought the Spanish and came back with a cargo of gold. Now look at her.'

Some of us looked up as we passed, all uncaring, and as we did so someone on the ship must have seen that we were a boatload of girls, for we heard shouts and men suddenly appeared from all over the decks, some shouting profanities, some declaring love, some pleading for us to break our journey and call in and see them.

Only one girl from our boat waved, and it certainly wasn't me, for I felt as if I didn't have a wave or smile left in me. On and on we went, until we came to deeper waters, a broader river and a mighty ship, spruce and newly painted.

'Is that our ship?' someone asked, but we were told we were not there yet, and it would be another hour's rowing (for we were going against the tide now) before we reached the ship we would be travelling on.

At last she was sighted.

''Tis the *Juanita*!' someone called out, holding a lantern aloft, and the rest of us sighed deeply, woke those who had been lucky enough to find sleep, and prepared ourselves to climb the ladder and go on board.

Chapter Twenty-One

Most of us were weeping as we trudged and shuffled down a passageway and into a small dark room. It was icy cold, and there was a strange aroma of salt and tar in the air which seemed to catch at the back of my throat.

One of the guards hooked a lantern over a beam, said in a mocking voice, 'I trust you'll sleep well, ladies!', and left us. We heard a crash as a bar came down outside the door, then the rattling of keys as he locked us in.

'Here!' shouted the girl who'd waved at the hulks – I'd heard her called Jane. 'Don't just go off and leave us. Where's our vittles?'

'You surely don't think they'll feed us at this time of the night!' said an older woman. 'We'll have to wait for morning.'

'Dumping us in here like a box of chickens!' Jane said, thumping at the door. 'At least in Newgate we were fed!'

The rest of us had been leaning against the walls and now began to slide to the floor, too tired and down-hearted to care whether we supped or starved. Betsy was practically asleep on her feet and I pulled her down beside me and put her head on my lap. There was a pile of threadbare blankets in the middle of the room and the older woman handed me one, with a wan smile, and helped me tuck it around Betsy. I remember thanking her, and this was the last thing I can recall before I fell asleep myself.

I woke to find Betsy shaking my arm and begging me to *please* wake up. I opened my eyes a little, but it was an effort.

'I am very, *very* hungry,' Betsy said. 'When will we get our bread?'

My eyelids drooped again. I felt stiff and bruised. My head ached with the lack of fresh air and the tarry smell was making me nauseous.

'Don't go back to sleep!' Betsy lifted my lids and held them open, then said in my ear, 'Are we in Australia yet?'

With many a groan and a sigh, I shifted myself into a sitting position. 'No, I'm very much afraid we are not – we haven't even started our journey.' Her lip wobbled at this. 'But soon we are going all the way down the river to the sea!' I said, trying to make it sound exciting.

'The sea.' She thought about this for some moments. 'But it's very large, and if we go there, however will my brother know how to find us?'

She hadn't spoken about Will for some time, so I wasn't expecting it and had to turn away so she wouldn't see the tears in my eyes. 'I'm not sure,' I said. After a moment, when I could trust my voice, I added, 'Maybe . . . maybe you and I will have to manage without him.'

'But I don't want to!' she said. 'You said we would find him if we came to London!'

'I know I did,' I said helplessly, and would have just dissolved into useless tears again but Cassandra, the mother of the only other child amongst us, asked Betsy if she wouldn't mind looking after her baby for a moment.

Betsy, more used to being looked after herself, was at first surprised and then took the child, who was about a year old, sat him on her hip and locked her arms around him as if she had been doing it all her life. For the moment, the question of Will was forgotten.

When a sailor appeared, rolling in a small barrel of fresh water for us, the girl called Jane spoke up loudly to demand the previous day's ration of meat, which she said was ours by rights. 'We surely should have had roast meat on Christmas Day!' she said indignantly. 'God knows we have little enough vittles the rest of the year.'

The sailor, a pigtailed man in baggy grey trousers, linen smock and neckerchief, stood looking at her, amused.

'I suppose you had the extra portions yourself,' she went on. 'You certainly look as if you have.'

I froze, thinking that she would be struck for her insolence, but to my surprise he roared with laughter. 'They said you were a bunch of disorderly wenches and you surely are!'

'Never mind that!' Jane said. 'Just enquire about our meat ration.'

'Yes, please do,' said the older woman, who gave her name as Margaret. 'And would you tell the captain that I am a lady born and bred, and there are certain privileges I should be allowed on board.'

I hid a gasp, thinking she was going to be hauled out for her rudeness, but the sailor just grinned. In due course, a smartly uniformed man appeared, telling us he was a warrant officer, and from him we learned everything that was going to happen, which struck us as very civil – and quite unlike how we had been treated by the turnkeys in Newgate.

He said that we would be moored on the River Thames past Woolwich – for that was where we were, and I had never heard of it – for several days while other girls sentenced to leave our shores came from nearby prisons. Once everyone was on board, the *Juanita* would sail down the Thames on the tide, go past the coast of Kent and around to Portsmouth Harbour to collect more women and provisions. After that, our final stop would be at Plymouth to collect girls from prisons at Exeter, Bristol and Taunton and take on livestock and fresh water before setting out for Botany Bay. This, apparently, was the place in Australia we were destined for.

'Although we will stop at several places to buy local foodstuffs and water,' the officer finished.

No one asked what these places were, and I certainly did not, for I hardly knew the names of the places in England, and the names of foreign countries would have meant little to me.

'If you all behave yourselves, we should have a fair journey,' he said. 'Our captain is a decent man and a gentleman, and there will be a surgeon and his assistant on board should anyone need medical attention.'

'What about telling our families where we've gone?' someone asked. 'What about our children? I had to leave three little ones in the care of my sister.'

'If you come and see me, we can make arrangements for letters to be sent,' said the officer. 'And if anyone's immediate family want to come and say goodbye, then a private cabin will be made available to them.'

Momentarily, I thought of my ma and pa getting my letter and of them trying to find me. They had no money for the journey to London, had never been on a coach, much less been to London, and they had no travelling clothes or bags. Even if they got as far as Charing Cross, how could they possibly find me, stuck on a ship they didn't know the name of, in the middle of nowhere, halfway to the sea?

'How many women will be sailing altogether?' Margaret asked.

'We will start with near two hundred,' he answered, and there were some gasps and shrieks at this, 'and it is our intention, with good care and fair conditions, to lose as few of you as possible. You are a valuable cargo.'

'Two hundred women!' someone said in shock. 'Surely there's not enough room.'

'The *Juanita* is a large vessel,' he said, 'and many of you can be accommodated on the orlop.' He must have seen our mystified faces, for he added, 'The orlop is the bottom deck, below the waterline, where you'll have your quarters. And I'd be obliged if you could learn some of the language of the ship: starboard, port, aft and bow and so forth.'

'But what about when we get there?' I enquired fearfully. 'What will happen to us then?'

'Are there wild animals?' someone else asked.

'None that you should worry about,' he said. 'It's a very beautiful country with wonderful mountains and lakes – and Botany Bay is a colony in dire need of women. You'll find yourselves much in demand.'

'I'm in demand every night on the Whitechapel Road!' Jane said and, though a few women laughed, I felt a chill run through me. It was surely going to be as Mrs Goodwin had predicted: we were being sent out there to marry the first man who propositioned us and bear his children whether we wanted to or not!

'But first things first,' he went on. 'Regulations state that you must all wash and disinfect yourselves, for there are several cases of gaol fever at Newgate and we must ensure that it's not brought on board.' He looked us over, one by one. 'Are there any of you who feel feverish or sick?'

We all shook our heads. 'Just damned hungry!' said Jane.

We were brought breakfast, which was not bread, but something called ship's biscuit: a dry disc made from flour and water and completely tasteless. After we'd eaten (and it proved near impossible to swallow more than two biscuits each), we were taken on deck, where someone had set up a blacksmith's anvil to sever the chains which held us together. We had to continue to wear the individual heavy shackles which locked around our calves, at least for the time being.

'These will be taken off when we're at sea, when there's no chance of you escaping,' the blacksmith told us.

In the daylight I could see the *Juanita* properly. The night before, in the darkness, it had been no more than shadows and shapes. But looking about me then I saw that it had three massive masts, each taller than the tallest tree I'd ever seen, and was altogether a miracle of ropes and rigging, each coil of rigging joined to the next and the whole seeming to be a gigantic puzzle. The sails were huge expanses of canvas that, just then, were rolled up and tied, but everyone said that open and filled with wind, they would be a magnificent sight. Magnificent they might be, I thought, but I didn't want to see them that way, for that would mean the ship had set sail and we were on our way to Botany Bay.

Not being chained together gave us a little more freedom – although we had precious little privacy to go with it, for the latrines we had to use during the day were merely planks with round holes cut in them, placed on each side of the deck so that the user could relieve herself directly into the sea. Most of us preferred this fresh air method to using the buckets supplied overnight.

The greatest treat for most of us was to be allowed to wash our hair and ourselves and to put on clean clothes and, it being high tide when we did so, we were permitted to use as much water as we liked. This was a mixture of sea-meets-the-river water pulled up in barrels and was probably not very clean – its only merit lay in the fact that there was plenty of it. A hard carbolic soap was provided, but I had to wash Betsy's hair four times before the water ran clean, and she did not hesitate to scream like a bantam all the while, so that I felt exhausted by the time I'd finished.

Our previous night's accommodation turned out to have been just a holding area for, once bathed and reasonably clean, we were taken to the orlop where, to our great surprise, there were already girls from other prisons and several children.

Things were a little awkward at first, for those who had been on the ship the longest seemed to think they had superiority over the rest of us, and had already taken the best positions on the sleeping shelves, as close as possible to a stove yet not too far from the hatches. They had set their possessions out and also begun to form their own little community, so it took a day or so of politeness on our part for there to begin to be the slightest thaw in their attitude.

How would it be, I wondered, once there were two hundred of us packed in nose to tail? At least at Newgate the population had been fluid: new girls had come in while others had gone out (or died) every day. Here, though, we would all be held together for a year or more; how long would it take for us all to be at each other's throats?

Over the next few days we began to get the feel of the ship and learned where we could and couldn't go. We were told that bare feet were safest for walking on the deck, but it was so icy that not many of us followed this advice. My feet were always aching with cold, but I'd managed to find two pieces of cardboard which, placed in the bottom of my shoes, covered up the holes in the soles and improved things slightly.

More worryingly, I discovered that I hated being shut in the orlop. It was underground – or, to be more precise, *underwater* – and there was no access to fresh air. Once you were inside it with the hatches closed there was a dreadful feeling of confinement. This didn't worry many of the girls, but I found it quite terrifying. It would be better once the ship was under way, we were told, for then we would be assigned jobs. We would help with the cleaning, cooking and washing, be responsible for the airing and care of our blankets and bedrolls, undertake the repairing of nets and sails, and scrub the decks. We learned most of this information from Margaret, who was not in the least bit afraid of our guards. She was the only one of us who had ever been on a ship before, for as a young woman she'd sailed to the Americas with her husband, an officer.

'Of course, I was in a very different position in those days,' she said. 'As the wife of one of the officers I ate at the captain's table.'

'But now you are down in the orlop with us!' Jane said bluntly. 'How did you come to fall so far?'

Margaret fluttered her hands. 'When my husband died, I had four young children to keep and no money. I was desperate. My children had not eaten for several days and so, after being contacted by a coiner, I passed on two gold sovereigns which had been tampered with. I was caught and served my time in prison, but learned a good deal there. When I came out, I formed a shoplifting partnership with another woman.'

'How did this work?' I asked.

'Well, my friend and I specialised in stealing expensive drapery,' she replied. 'We would dress up very fine, go to one of the big shops and ask to see some brocade or embroidered fabric. I would remark that a titled lady I knew had recommended the shop, and this pleased the assistants and allayed their fears. We'd then purchase a small sample of the material, and when the assistant went to wrap it, take a bale off the shelf and throw it into a large pocket I had especially made in my petticoats. Of course, it was the devil of a job to walk with such a bulky amount of fabric banging against my legs, but I only had to take it as far as the nearest pawnbroker's.' We laughed. 'Of course, the change in fashions rather hindered our exploits. Believe me when I say that it's impossible to hide a bale of linen under a straight slip of muslin.'

'So was this the end of your shoplifting?' someone asked.

Margaret shook her head. 'We merely adapted our methods. We would take a bale of material to the light in order to see the colour better, and I would distract the assistant while my friend slipped out of the door with it. We worked around the Kentish towns for a year or more like this.'

'But how did you get caught?' I asked.

'Ah,' she said, 'on the final occasion my friend and I worked together, she was seen and pursued down the road by the manager. She threw the material over the nearest wall and it went straight into an ornamental pond.' She rolled her eyes. 'What a to-do it caused: the fabric was eighteen shillings a yard and we caused twenty-seven yards to be ruined!'

Margaret sighed and then looked around at us. 'Well, you are all looking very fine,' she said after a moment, and we primped our hair and smiled at this, for nearly all of us had made full use of the washing facilities and most were wearing the gowns which Mrs Fry had supplied. These were somewhat creased and crumpled, but at least were clean. 'There is one thing you should be aware of,' she went on. 'It is a long voyage and the sailors may make certain demands on you along the way.'

'Well, if they do 'tis nothing to me!' Jane cried.

'If you accept these demands,' Margaret said, ignoring her, 'it may mean an easier journey: you'll have better sleeping quarters and may, perhaps, obtain more rations. However, you must remember that you may well find yourself bearing a child before the end of the journey.'

Those of us who had been smiling at Jane's words stopped.

'Remember that your sailor, be he an officer or an ordinary seaman, will be sailing away again, while you, and perhaps a child, will not. You will find yourself still a prisoner, but in a strange country with an infant to care for too.'

I hadn't thought of this, and it took me aback somewhat. I certainly did not want either a sailor or a child! Betsy was enough for me – more than enough, for I worried constantly about keeping her fed and warm and safe. What to do, though? If you were selected by a sailor, would you be able to say yes or no to him? Probably not, I thought. Like being chosen by a prisoner in Botany Bay, it was *they* who would do the choosing.

Unless I got away before we sailed.

The next time I was on deck I studied the landscape around me carefully, wondering about those men that the guards had spoken of who'd got away from the hulks. If anyone was going to escape, I thought, it would have to be soon, before the ship started on its interminable journey. But how could such a thing be managed? The small rowing boats on the deck were tied up as tightly as parcels with knotted ropes and tarpaulin and, even if I could somehow procure one, how would I get it into the water? Alternatively, if I went over the side and tried to swim to shore there was no habitation nearby, no houses to make for, no markers to indicate where the land began. Exactly where *was* the shore, anyway? Where did the deep, muddy water blend into marsh and the marsh become solid? A girl on her own would surely perish out there in the freezing waters. And besides, I was not on my own, for I had Betsy.

No, it was clearly impossible. I would have to bear it: I would have to bid goodbye to my country, my family, and to all those in England I loved.

Chapter Twenty-Two

We were four days at Woolwich: four days in which more girls, women and children arrived, dull-eyed and bewildered in barges and rowing boats, until we numbered about eighty. I continued to loathe being confined in the orlop, for it was low-ceilinged and stuffy, and its lack of any natural light meant it always had to be lit with foul-smelling tallow candles. Moving around, I'd often hit my head on the low beams and, hearing the great bolts being pushed across at night, would feel strangely panicked, for I feared that seawater would seep in through the gigantic timbers and creep higher and higher until it came over our heads. When morning arrived and the hatches were opened I was always awake and the first to go up the ladder on to the deck. Fair weather or foul, I felt better in the open air.

On the morning of the fourth day our biscuit allowance was sent down to us as usual, but the hatches were not opened. They wanted us out of the way, said one of the seamen, because at midday we were due to sail with the tide around the coast towards Portsmouth. Before that, however, another group of girls arrived from Newgate and went through the washing and cleansing process just as we had done. When they were allowed to join the rest of us, I was overjoyed to discover that Martha was amongst them, accompanied by Robyn and baby Elizabeth.

All three were crying pitifully when they were brought on board, and Martha told me that they had had a particularly onerous journey from Newgate. They had set off the day before but a woman, previously quite well, had been taken with sickness on the boat down, so that after two hours they'd had to turn back. In all, they had been travelling for fourteen hours.

'Gaol fever used to be a summer thing,' Martha said, collapsing beside me in the orlop, 'but now 'tis no respecter of seasons. Fever is spreading right across Newgate – the Master's Side as well as the Commons'. I could not wait to leave and bring the children to safety.'

'But how was it that the court passed sentence on you so quickly?' I asked. 'I thought the shop manager was not to be found.'

'At first he was not.' She managed to smile and added, 'But then he came forward to indict me and was arrested for bigamy for his trouble, so that he must stand trial himself.' So saying, she closed her eyes, exhausted, and

Margaret took baby Elizabeth from her and banged on the hatch for one of the sailors to bring a bowl of bread and warm milk, and quickly, for there was a nursing mother on board.

Betsy, beaming to see her friend, greeted her and then began pointing out the various parts of the ship. 'The *port* is this side, Robyn,' I heard her say (getting it wrong), 'and the other side is the *starrybird*. You must remember that.'

'Port and starrybird,' Robyn repeated obediently.

'The front of the boat is the *stern*,' we heard as they walked off, 'and the back of the boat is the *aft* . . .'

'I thought you were never going to accept a sentence which took you away from England,' I said to Martha when she had recovered slightly. 'Although I'm mighty pleased that you did!'

'I was going to refuse. But when they said my choice was to stay in Newgate and risk gaol fever, or be transported, I knew which I should choose.' She smiled a little. 'Besides, realising that we were to be on the same ship, I knew I would have a friend.'

I smiled. 'I am *very* glad to see you,' I said, giving her a hug.

When the tide was right, the *Juanita* set sail through the counties of Essex and Kent towards the open sea. The wind was high, and even down on the bottom deck we could hear it buffeting, filling the sails, the masts creaking and cracking. Shut in the orlop in the semi-darkness,

I began to feel off balance and ill. Several other women felt the same.

''Tis just seasickness,' I was told as I sprawled on the floor, retching. 'You'll soon get used to it.'

'*Just* seasickness?' I muttered, giddy and nauseous.

'The ship is barely moving!' said Jane, who was hardly affected. 'Wait until we reach the high seas!'

I groaned.

'Shall I stroke your forehead?' Betsy asked.

'No, go away and play,' I said weakly, then was sick in a bucket and slept until the ship reached Portsmouth.

Martha told me later that I had missed a session of storytelling, for, locked up together for several hours, the girls had begun speaking of the crimes which had caused them to be there. One had taken receipt of a pair of shoe buckles knowing them to have been stolen; another had cut eight brass buttons from a man's coat. Several were there for coining, and – although originally sentenced to hang – had had their sentences commuted to transportation as a thanksgiving for the King having briefly recovered his senses. One girl had bought and resold the skins of swans (which was a royal bird and so seen as treason); another had made away with a line of sheets that had been blowing on the line in a laundress's garden; yet another had stolen a pocket watch and gold chain from a gentleman while he was being shaved at his barber's. Several pairs of girls had, like Margaret and her friend, worked together to relieve shopkeepers of their stock and one resourceful girl had 'bonneted' a man. This, Martha explained, meant that she, sitting high on a wall, had pushed a passing man's top hat right down over his eyes. Whilst he was temporarily blinded, she had robbed him of the large Parmesan cheese he was taking home from market.

'Some of those crimes were ingenious,' Martha told me – not without some admiration. 'If ever I fall upon hard times again, I shall certainly try bonneting.'

Once our ship was at anchor, I felt a little better. This relief was tempered, however, by the knowledge that very shortly I would have no respite at all from seasickness. The ghastly nausea, once begun, would go on for days and weeks and months on end. No wonder, I thought, that so many died on long sea journeys.

Several girls joined us from the gaols in and around Portsmouth, so that we numbered near one hundred and fifty. There would be one more stop at Plymouth, then we would be on our way to Botany Bay. Thinking of this, I stood on the deck staring at the green landscape before me, at the hedges and fields and trees, trying to impress them on my mind, until they became smudged with tears and I could see no more.

Sitting on the deck with Martha a little later, we watched the ship's rowing boats going backwards and forwards to the shore bringing provisions for the journey. So much food: types of vegetables I had never seen before, cabbages and green-stuffs growing in vast wooden trays, sacks of grain, flour and sugar, wood for the kitchen range, coal for the braziers, sacks of carrots and potatoes. To carry these provisions, temporary shacks had been built for storage in the centre of the main deck.

When darkness fell we were confined below as usual. We got little sleep, however, for Martha's baby was tetchy and cried for several hours, and this poor infant's wailing joined in jarring chorus with a hammering and a sawing which echoed across the ship and went on most of the night. In the morning when the hatches went back and we were allowed on deck, I was happy (I say happy, but 'twas not happiness, only a slight lessening of the gloom I felt) to see that animal pens had been constructed, and to know that at Plymouth we would be taking livestock on board. This, of course, only meant one thing to me: cows – and I vowed to discover who had overall care of them and ask if I could help with their milking. If I didn't manage to get off the ship, I thought, at least the cows might help keep me sane.

We sailed along to Plymouth, which was but a short journey, though still enough to make me queasy. We were to anchor here for a week, we were told, and once I was on deck I sought a quiet corner where I could wait for the cows to come on board. Martha joined me, and looking around us we marvelled at the huge number of tall ships moored on the banks, some glossy and magnificent, some with their hulls splintered or masts broken, others looking weather-beaten and worn. England, I knew, was at war with Napoleon, and there were many boats in the harbour waiting to be repaired or repainted.

A crate of chickens was carried up the gangplank, all squawking loudly, and I wondered to myself what would happen to the crate they were brought in. Would it go back to the farmer, or be used on board as firewood? If it went back to the farmer, what if someone was hiding inside it?

There *must* be a way to escape, I thought, or this was like to be the last I ever saw of my native land! I would never see my mother or father again, never make my peace with Miss Alice, never find out what had happened to Will. Before I knew it I was weeping again, and this time it fell to Martha to try and comfort *me*.

I'd dried my tears by the time Jane joined us. 'I've been told that there are some new young officers coming on board!' she said. 'This is the best place to see them.'

Martha – who had soon got the measure of Jane – said, 'Officers? You seem to set yourself very high.'

'Indeed I do!' Jane said, and when the next young man in uniform came across the gangplank she called over to say that she had a speck in her eye.

'Then ask one of your sisters to remove it,' came the reply, 'for a woman's touch is more gentle than any that I can provide.'

'Not more gentle than you could be, I am sure!' Jane called back.

Embarrassed at her forwardness, I looked to see how the young man had taken this, then, horrified, ducked down so I was out of his view. It was the young naval officer I'd last seen in Bridgeford – Miss Sophia's beau!

Chapter Twenty-Three

I wondered after why I had ducked down, for it was nothing to me whether he was on the ship or not, and I doubted if he would have recognised me anyway.

'What a *most* attractive fellow!' Jane said, staring after him brazenly. 'An officer, too. And him not above one and twenty, I'll bet.' She turned to me and Martha. 'He's standing by the gangplank with a midshipman. Do look and tell me if I'm not right!'

Martha sat up and looked across the deck but I did not, pretending interest in a game that Robyn and Betsy were playing. Jane called over to the nearest sailor to ask who the officer was, and was told that he was Lieutenant Mackenzie Warwick, an assistant surgeon, on his third posting overseas.

Mackenzie Warwick was a good, strong name, I mused, and I wondered if Miss Sophia was still enamoured of him. I decided that she probably was, for he was a handsome man, gallant and (I knew from my meeting with him) well mannered, and Miss Sophia was the kind of girl who, having fallen in love once, would see no necessity to fall out of it. Realising this, I thought to myself that I was probably that sort of girl, too, for my dreams were all of Will and the time we'd had together, and it felt to me that he was the only one I would ever be in love with.

All day we sat on the deck, well out of the way, and watched while various livestock came on board: chickens, ducks, rabbits, pigs, sheep, geese, goats – although no cows as yet. The chickens would lay eggs throughout the voyage and be eaten once they stopped laying. The rest of the animals would just breed and be eaten – although the cows, of course, would not suffer this fate unless they went dry. More seamen joined the ship, too: a brace of officers, some midshipmen, young boys to climb the rigging, and ordinary sailors with a golden ring in their ear.

It was a day when we girls were pretty much ignored and, while the ship was being prepared for its long voyage, I spent my time thinking of home. Home: both Bridgeford Hall and the little cottage I'd grown up in.

'Are you quite resigned to going to a strange country now?' I asked Martha, for I'd heard no more about her fears of being eaten up by fierce animals or having to fend for herself in alien landscapes.

'I am,' she said. 'And I have thought long about it and am even prepared to marry a man I don't love.'

'Never!'

'Yes, I am, Kitty,' she said very seriously. 'And you should be, too. The important thing is that the man you marry should have a trade, a cottage and a piece of land.'

'But not to love him!'

'Tush! We will have roofs over our heads, and our children will be cared for. In London I never knew where my next bowl of soup was coming from, let alone where we would lay our heads at night.'

'Then would you not . . .' I lowered my voice, '. . . think of escaping?'

'Escaping from this ship?' She laughed and pointed to our shackles. 'Of course not. How could anyone do that?'

'There must be a way!' I said urgently. 'I heard the sailors talking of two men who went over the side of a hulk a while back.'

'Went over the side and drowned, I'll warrant. And they were two *men*, Kitty. Men are stronger than us. Men can suffer hardships and fight their way out of places. Men can swim.'

'I can swim a little,' I said, remembering how Will had taught me.

'Not in that water! It would be cold enough to kill you,' she said, shuddering.

'Perhaps . . .'

'Kitty, I'd rather have the promise of a husband and cottage than go over the side. And suppose you were saved and recaptured? What extra penalty would you suffer?'

I went quiet, for this thought had already occurred to me.

Thinking of my swimming lessons with Will, I was reminded of the note Lieutenant Warwick had written to Miss Sophia, and eventually I determined that I must inform him that she had never received it. He might have been waiting for a reply from her all this time and, when it hadn't arrived, decided that she didn't love him – and I was sure this wasn't the case.

While I was thinking of how I could best secure an appointment with him, an opportunity – albeit an unhappy one – presented itself. Melody, a little girl who'd done nothing but weep since arriving on the ship, fell into a deep sleep from which it proved impossible to rouse her. Margaret asked for a surgeon or physician to attend, and it was Lieutenant Warwick who came. I found out later that he'd been assigned to look after the women, while a more senior surgeon would care for the captain and crew.

Sadly, he pronounced that little could be done.

'The very fact that she has not eaten or drunk since coming on board is enough to foretell her death,' he said. 'But I will have her moved to the infirmary and keep a watch there.'

'Is there anything we can do to aid her?' Margaret asked.

He shrugged. 'Perhaps chafe her hands and feet to try and bring some heat to them.'

He left, and I followed him up the ladder and out of the orlop.

'Excuse me, sir,' I said, when he made to go into the officers' quarters. 'May I speak with you a moment?'

He turned. 'What is it?'

'I fear you don't remember me.'

He looked at me uncomprehendingly. 'I don't believe so.'

'I was the milkmaid at Bridgeford Hall, sir.'

Startled, he looked at me again and nodded. 'I do remember you – although you have changed somewhat since then. But what are you doing on this ship?'

I shook my head. 'It is too long to tell, sir. I went to London on an errand for Miss Alice and . . .' my eyes filled with ready tears, '. . . and it all went wrong for me.'

'For you and these many other girls,' he said, waving around the ship. 'But perhaps you can make a fresh start in Botany Bay.' He took a step, then turned back. 'But would you mind telling me if you have any news of your mistress?' he asked in a low voice. 'How fares Miss Sophia? Is she well?'

'Sir, it was she I came to talk to you about.'

'Is she . . . betrothed?'

I shook my head. 'No, sir. Not to my knowledge. But you remember the last time I saw you, you gave me a message for her.'

'I do remember. A message she never replied to.'

'Indeed, sir. She could not reply because she never received it.'

'*What?*' he said.

I shook my head. There was no need, I had already

decided, for him to know of my carelessness at letting the message fall to pieces in the river. 'When I got back to the hall with it that evening, I found that Miss Sophia had already been sent away.'

He gasped. 'So that's why she didn't come to me as I asked!'

'She was sent away to her uncle in Bath,' I said. 'She travelled there under the supervision of her aunt, and wasn't to be allowed to return to Bridgeford Hall until the new year.'

'Oh! So she never knew I had written asking her to go away with me?'

I shook my head. 'She did not.'

'And because she didn't come, I presumed she didn't . . .' And his final two words were only a murmur.

'I'm so sorry, sir.'

'Was there any further news of her before you left?' he asked eagerly.

I shook my head again. 'Only that Miss Alice and Milord and Lady went to visit her, and she refused to be introduced to a young Army officer of their choosing.'

A little smile creased his lips. 'Then there might still be a chance for me. Even if she is still in Bath, I could write a letter to await her return to Bridgeford.'

'You could, sir,' I said, and did not have the heart to tell him that, whether she had already arrived home or not, Lord or Lady Baysmith would probably seize the letter and have it destroyed.

He sighed. 'But I will be a year out on the *Juanita*, and a year home. Will she wait for me, do you think?'

'I'm afraid I couldn't say, sir,' I said as gently as possible. How could anyone know such a thing?

I went back to Martha and told her all that had happened and she, though admitting it was thrillingly romantic, said that she was of the opinion that a young girl of good family should always be guided by her mother and father.

Melody died that evening and her body was moved from the infirmary to the chaplain's cabin to await burial at sea. Margaret told me that there had been another death that same night, a woman who had died of gaol fever, whose body was to be buried at the same time. The authorities at the port were insisting, because of the risk of the highly contagious fever spreading, that these rites should be carried out at sea.

'There will be many more deaths amongst us before we reach Australia,' Margaret said. ''Tis a sad fact, but true.'

I spent a while dwelling on her words, looking around and wondering who would be next to fall ill and die, but then something happened which took my mind entirely away from such things.

I received a note.

One of the children brought the note to me: a little girl named Hope, newly arrived at the ship from one of the West Country gaols with her mother.

'A man gave me a ha'penny to bring it,' she said, holding the shiny coin and staring at it in wonder.

'A man. You mean a sailor?' I asked.

She nodded.

'What was he like?'

She shrugged, as if to say that they all looked the same.

'Did he know my name?'

She shook her head. 'He pointed at you. He said to give it to the girl in the grey dress with wavy hair.'

As Hope ran off, I was minded to throw away the small, folded missive without reading it, for one of our girls had received a note from a sailor the day before which had contained a number of crude suggestions.

Martha smiled at me. 'You have caught the eye of someone fine, I'll be bound.'

'Someone fine would use a quill and parchment!' I said, for the note was written in pencil on the meanest scrap of paper.

'It is surely not that officer,' said Jane, rather disgruntled, for she had spoken of little but Lieutenant Warwick since setting eyes on him.

'No, of course it isn't,' I said, and thought of the contrast between the groomed and fragrant Miss Sophia and myself, and smiled. I was torn between screwing up the slip of paper or throwing it overboard, but curiosity got the better of me.

'Meet me by the first lifeboat after dark.' I read it out to the girls around me, and was rewarded by some gasps and giggles.

' 'Tis but a joke,' I said. 'For certain I'm not going.'

'Why ever not?' Jane asked.

'Because I don't want any Jack tar sailor to try and tumble me!'

'Ha! Hoity-toity!' she said. 'He might be a good and comely fellow.'

'You may go instead then.'

'I thank you, but I can find my own sweetheart,' she said pertly.

When I went up on deck, I threw the paper over the side. I did ask Hope later if she could describe the sailor who'd given it to her, but she could tell very little, only said that he was 'tall and dark' – which description applied to near every man on board.

'For as much as it has pleased Almighty God to take unto himself the souls of our sisters here departed, we therefore commit their bodies to the deep, in sure and certain hopes of the resurrection to eternal life . . .'

As the chaplain stood at the side of the ship intoning the words of the funeral service, a few girls watched from the top deck. There weren't many of us, for we were now only too aware of the proximity of death and most did not need reminders of how it was lurking in wait for us.

The service over, we saw Lieutenant Warwick being rowed off into the morning mist with an oarsman and two bodies – those of Melody and the girl who'd died of gaol fever – sewn into shrouds of canvas. We were rather subdued after that.

A further note arrived for me later that day. And yet another the following morning, saying the same thing, addressed to me by name (though spelled with an I at the end: Kitti) and stuck in the top of the hatch.

'He has discovered your name!' said Martha.

''Tis not hard. He would only have to ask one of the children,' I said.

However, I spoke to Betsy and Robyn later, and they said no one had asked them anything. I could not help but be intrigued. I didn't want to start a liaison with anyone, but I did want to know who was writing to me. What if I stayed hidden on deck, I thought, just to look at the fellow? It was vain of me, I knew, but I was flattered by this mystery man's attentions, for it had been a very long time since anyone had taken the slightest notice of me.

When dusk came, then, and they rang the bell for us to go down to the orlop, I asked Martha if she would see Betsy settled to sleep, while I stayed, hidden, on the deck. When it got dark I crept (undercover and holding on to the manacle around my legs to prevent it from clanking) not to the first lifeboat, but to a hidey-hole I'd come upon behind a gigantic coil of rope. From here, by the light of the oil lamp hanging above the gangplank, I could see if anyone came to the meeting place.

The ship was rocking gently, the sea plashing against the sides, and I fear that, after an hour or so, and despite the carousing coming from the crew's quarters, I fell asleep. When I woke up, it was to feel that someone had one hand across my mouth whilst the other was holding my two wrists in a tight grip.

Terrified, I began struggling. The person who held me was behind me and in shadow, so I could only see the shape of him.

'Are you Kitty?' he asked in a low, gruff voice.

I nodded, shivering with fear.

'Why have you come here?' he asked, then loosened his grip around my mouth a little, so that I could reply.

'I . . . I received some notes,' I babbled. 'Someone asked me to meet him.'

He began to say something in reply, but I seized the opportunity to sink my teeth into the hand that was around my mouth. He let go of my wrists with an oath, and I jerked around to look him in the face.

It was Will.

Chapter Twenty-Four

I had oft thought of what I'd say and how I'd act if I ever saw Will again, and it was then that I found out. My first reaction was one of total fury, and I turned on him like a wildcat.

'How dare you! How could you?' I hissed through gritted teeth, flailing my arms and trying to punch and scratch him. 'You are the most heartless and wicked devil that ever walked this earth!'

'Hush! Hush!' came the only reply.

'I will not hush!' I kicked at him in the darkness. 'I will put it about that you tried to kill me!'

'Kitty –'

'I'll have you taken to Newgate! I'll see that you hang!'

'Quiet!'

I managed to reach his face and scratch it. 'I'll have you put in irons.'

'Kitty,' he said quietly. 'I am already in irons.'

I stopped my tirade.

'See.' He caught hold of my hand and put it on his calf, so I could feel that he was wearing manacles.

I straightened up, squinting under the dim light of the lantern high above, and stared at him. It was the same Will, but thinner, browner, his hair scraped back in a pigtail like that of the sailors, a red kerchief around his neck and a new little white scar in a vertical line through his lip. The fact that he was in manacles meant little to me then, for I was still intent on killing him.

'You are beyond wicked!' I said, so choked with fury that I could hardly get the words out. 'Betsy and I could both be dead for all you care! You left us – *left us . . .*' And then I could manage no more before I broke down completely.

He put his arms around me while I pounded my fists against his chest.

'I will never, ever forgive you,' I said, shaking all over. 'You left me with Betsy, and we came to London to find you, and then I was taken to Newgate, which was terrible in the extreme, and now we're here and set for Australia and I will never see my mother and father or my home again!'

'Kitty, listen to me: I was *pressed.*'

This meant nothing to me. 'What do you mean?' I asked between sobs.

'I mean I was taken away by Royal Navy men and pressed into service. I am just as much a captive as you are. That's why I'm wearing manacles.'

I stared at him but was not prepared to give an inch. 'I don't understand. What happened to you?'

He sat down beside the coil of rope and I sat beside him, but it was a while before he started speaking.

'It was at the end of August,' he began at length. 'I took two Navy fellows across the river to Millbridge in the normal way, and they complimented me on the way I handled the boat and said they had need of such strong young men in the Navy.'

'But you surely didn't . . . ?'

'Of course I didn't! I thanked them, and they asked if I was a single man or no.'

'And you said . . . ?'

'I said I was a single man, but had certain responsibilities. When I'd taken them over I said I would sit in the boat and wait to row them back if they wished, and they asked if I would first join them for a tankard of ale at the Royal Oak and drink the King's health. I refused at first, but they persisted, and were such civil fellows that I thought they might take it as an insult if I didn't join them.'

'And then?'

'Then we went to the Royal Oak. I took up my ale and we drank to the King, to the Royal Navy and to the right outcome of the wars, and when I got to the bottom I saw there was a silver coin there.'

I looked at him curiously. 'Why? What did that mean?'

'I will tell you. I drained the tankard and took up the coin, and when I did so both men cheered and said I had taken the King's shilling and was now in the Royal

Navy. I protested, but to no avail, for they clapped handcuffs on me. They rowed me back to my hut to collect my tin box and spare clothing and so on, and that night we left for Plymouth Sound in a closed carriage.'

I looked at him bleakly. 'But was there *nothing* you could do?'

'There was not, for I was in handcuffs and the two fellows whose charge I was in were sturdily built. I was fair desperate to leave you a message at the hut, believe me.'

'If only you had!'

He sighed. 'Never have I regretted so much the fact that I couldn't write. There was not even paper or pencil in my hut, or I might have drawn a picture telling you what had happened. I was fair out of my mind trying to think of what to do.' His voice thickened. 'It broke my heart to think of you and Betsy finding me gone; of you hating me or thinking I was dead.'

'Both of those things and more,' I said, but I gripped his hands tightly, for the tables had turned and now I was comforting him. After a moment I asked, 'But what happened to you after that?'

'We went to Plymouth, picking up some other fellows on the way who'd been similarly taken. Once there we worked in the dockyards, but always manacled and under close guard.'

'What did you do all day?'

He shrugged. 'Repaired rigging, sewed nets, scrubbed

tables, caught rats, practised our letters. That's how I could write those notes to you.'

'Did *you* write the notes you sent?'

He nodded.

'You spelled my name wrongly.'

'That's how it sounds,' he said, smiling.

We stared at each other for a moment, nose to nose, and I felt I wanted to turn cartwheels like a child, or race about or scream – anything that might help express the turmoil inside me.

'A dozen pressed men were packed off to help fight Napoleon, but myself and some others were – by all that's wonderful – chosen to work below decks on the *Juanita* and help sail her to Botany Bay.' He gave a short laugh. 'They say that when we get out to sea we may have our shackles off. What they don't know is that I've already devised a way to spring the lock open with my penknife.'

I sighed very deeply, still not really accepting or believing that he hadn't left me through choice, but was actually here, beside me. 'When did you find out that Betsy and I were on board?'

'Two days ago,' he said, smoothing my hair back from my face as he spoke. 'When I saw you I could not believe it . . . just could not believe my eyes.'

'Tell me what happened!' I urged.

'Well, we had heard which ship we were to travel on: the word had spread around the yard that we would be going to Botany Bay with . . .' he raised his eyebrows, '. . . a cargo of disgraced and disorderly women.'

'Not *all* of us so,' I put in swiftly.

'We spoke long into the night about such women and there was much bawdy talk and jesting.'

'I'm sure . . .' I blushed at the thought of what might have been said about us.

'And then we pressed men were taken on board and sent down below, so we hardly got a glimpse of anyone. But when I was sent on deck to collect something, I saw you and Betsy seated near the gangplank watching the livestock come on board.'

'And what did you think when you saw us?'

'I thought you were a mirage,' he said simply. 'I saw you there and wondered if I might have gone mad.'

'But why didn't you shout? Why didn't you let us know?'

'That was my first instinct, but then I realised that I should not let anyone discern that there was a link between us.'

'Why?'

'Because I've been trying to devise an escape plan for some time.' I gasped at this and he continued, 'Now, of course, my plans will include you and Betsy, which will make it a shade more difficult.'

'I must tell Betsy you're here!' I said.

'Not yet! If you tell her she won't be able to keep it to herself.' He took my hand. 'But tell me how you and Betsy came to be in a cargo of girls being sent to Botany Bay.'

'We are *both* here because the authorities – that is, the

judge and the prison governor and so on – think that Betsy is my own child.'

He looked baffled at this. 'They think that Betsy is yours?'

I nodded. 'I had to say that to save us from being separated, otherwise they might have taken Betsy and put her in an orphanage.'

He heaved a sigh. 'Then although I am still bewildered as to how all this happened, I thank you from the bottom of my heart for looking after her. Betsy and I both owe you a great deal. When I think I could have lost her for ever . . .'

We sat speechless for a few moments – and I think both of us were trying to come to terms with all that had happened – then he took my other cold hand in his own. 'But tell me how you came to be here? What were you convicted of? For it surely is the most wonderful thing that we've ended up in the same place.'

'I will tell you everything,' I said, and took him through the whole story: how I'd believed he was in London working with his cousins, so when the opportunity had presented itself for me to go there, I'd done so, and there met with my great misfortune. I told him about my realisation that half of London could see St Paul's, about the rogue of a landlord and the kindness of Mr Holloway, about the horror of Newgate Gaol – the cold and the stink and the fierceness of the inmates, and tears fell from two pairs of eyes during the course of all this telling.

Oblivious of the cold, we talked all night, until my account of what had happened had reached the present day and the fact that Miss Sophia's beau was on board. As dawn streaked the sky in the east and we prepared to part, he impressed upon me both the need for secrecy and for us to act with all speed, for the day which was dawning was Tuesday, and on Wednesday at high tide the *Juanita*, with or without us, would set sail for Botany Bay.

Chapter Twenty-Five

Will went down below and I stayed out of sight until the hatches were opened and the other girls began coming up the ladder. Martha appeared with the children and I kissed Betsy, then – on Martha saying she was desperate to know what had happened – put my finger to my lips and said I would tell her as soon as we found ourselves alone. Martha had become a good friend and, though Will had urged restraint upon me, it would have been impossible not to tell her about this.

The other girls milled around us, finding spaces to sit or beginning their work on repairing lengths of canvas, scrubbing decks or gutting fish. There would be work for all once we'd set sail, we'd been told, but until then it was only those girls who had received longer sentences who worked. Their duties were always outside and their hands, with almost continuous exposure to cold and salt water, had become red-raw. This caused some of them to be resentful of the rest of us, which manifested itself in certain spiteful ways: tripping another girl on the deck ladder, giving the odd sly pinch, stealing food when a girl's back was turned. Martha and I had spoken about it and concluded that it would not take long for an almighty fight to break out.

That morning we waited, playing with baby Elizabeth (who, despite her surroundings, had recently begun to smile), until we found ourselves with space to speak more freely. The cows came on board during the time we were waiting, being swung over on giant hammocks from another ship, but I felt so anxious and overwrought that I hardly glanced their way. What were these cows to me, when I might soon be seeing my own?

'You must promise not to say a word!' I began to Martha at last.

'Of course I won't! Was it someone handsome who sent the notes?'

'It was. But more than that . . .' I lowered my voice, 'it was someone I knew from home: my sweetheart who had disappeared.'

'The one who left you to come to London?' she said, her voice rising indignantly.

I nodded.

'Then I'm very surprised that you would have anything to do with him. Why did he run off and leave you?'

'He didn't leave voluntarily,' I said. 'He was taken away. Pressed.'

'Ah . . .' she breathed, obviously knowing what this meant. 'Poor lad.'

'He still intends that we should be together, Martha! He says he is going to make a plan for us to escape.'

'Escape from this ship?' She shook her head. 'Then I wish you a great deal of luck.' She nodded towards the gangplank, which was the ship's only point of exit and entry and guarded around the clock by two hefty sailors. 'We sail tomorrow. How can an escape be managed in that short time?'

I shook my head. 'I don't know.'

'And what might happen to you if you're retaken?'

'I don't know,' I said again. 'I just have to trust him.'

She took my hand, looking at me sadly. 'If you escape, I shall miss you very much,' she said.

'I'm sorry that you can't come with us . . .'

She shook her head. ''Tis a kind thought, but I am quite resigned to going to Australia now. Besides, I have caught the eye of a midshipman.'

'Already!'

'Things move fast at sea,' she said, blushing.

Deciding I must do something to keep my mind occupied, Martha and I went to see the six newly arrived cows, and I was a little saddened to realise that one of the poor beasts must have had her calf taken away from her too early, for she was lowing piteously and looking towards the shore. The cows were Friesians, from the Low Countries, handsome in form and known for their good milk yield. They were resilient, too, and would have to be, for we were told by a sailor that, in high seas, they'd be tied up tightly and lashed to the masts. It would not do for one sixth of the ship's allowance of milk and beef to slip overboard.

That morning the last women had arrived from Exeter Gaol (a sorry bunch, ill dressed for cold weather and most forlorn) and the *Juanita* had taken delivery of some crates of lemons and limes that she'd been waiting for. I hardly knew what I did all that day; my mind was jumping all over the place with fear and possibilities. The lack of sleep meant that I felt strange and light-headed, but I was reluctant to close my eyes in case I missed Will coming by with a message.

I counted the hours as the ship's bell sounded, each hour bringing us a little closer to the time the ship would sail.

By mid-afternoon I was near despair, for no message had come from Will and I feared either that an officer had found out he was planning to escape, or that he'd been moved to another ship. Another hour went by and one of the little cabin boys came by and pressed a note in my hand asking me to go to the water butt on the star-board side without delay.

I told Martha where I was going and made my way there as quickly as I could, my heart racing. Finding Will still seemed much like a miracle, although we couldn't touch, or even look as if we were speaking to each other; he pretended to be cleaning the iron mugs which hung on chains around the water butt, while I stared out to the fields beyond the city, as if bidding a sad farewell to my country.

'I couldn't contact you before, Kitty,' he said in a whisper. 'I had duties to attend to down below.'

'What are we going to do?' I asked with some urgency. 'I've been thinking and thinking . . .'

'As I have, for what I'd planned for myself will no longer work with three.'

A sailor passed by and checked some rigging, but didn't give either of us a glance.

'But now I've devised another plan,' Will said. His eyes met mine. 'How brave do you feel?'

'Brave?' I asked, pulling my shawl over my head against a sudden gust of wind. 'I don't feel brave at all.'

'Then how much do you want to return home?'

I tried to speak, but a lump rose in my throat so that I just stared at him.

He nodded and touched my hand. 'As much as I,' he said quietly. 'Then this is what you have to do . . .'

Chapter Twenty-Six

❋

On Wednesday at dusk I heard, from far above me on the deck of the *Juanita*, the voice of the chaplain: '*For as much as it has pleased Almighty God to take unto himself the souls of our sisters here departed . . .*'

I could not see anything, for I was in darkness, but knew that if I could, there would be a few girls – Martha amongst them – standing at the side of the ship, looking down at my canvas-wrapped body lying in the bottom of a rowing boat.

'I must not move . . . I must not move . . .' I heard Betsy say in a whisper.

It was noisy, thank goodness: seawater plashing against the sides of the ship, shouts from other craft, the sound of a sea shanty being sung on a nearby boat.

'No, you mustn't move,' I whispered in her ear, for she was lying close beside me inside my canvas shroud. 'And you mustn't speak either. Not for a little while.'

'I must not move and I must not speak,' came Betsy's muffled voice. 'I must not . . .'

'. . . *we therefore commit their bodies to the deep, in sure and certain hopes of the resurrection to eternal life . . .*'

I felt something light land on top of me and knew what it was. 'I will make sure that you have a flower on your coffin,' Martha had said to me, and she'd pulled a velvet rose from the front of the gown given to her by Mrs Fry. 'Even if you are not really dead, you must have a flower.'

The chaplain intoned a final blessing and there was an answering 'Amen' from Martha and the few girls standing on board the ship.

'Thank you, Chaplain,' I heard Lieutenant Warwick call to him, and then, 'If you please, sailor!' to Will, who was rowing us.

Will loosed the rope that was keeping him at the side of the ship and began to row away from it. Almost immediately, lying in the hull of the rowing boat and sewn into a canvas coffin bag, I began to feel sick from the rise and fall of the waves. I would have to tolerate it, however, because we didn't know for how long anyone might be watching us. We had to get as far away from the *Juanita* and the other Royal Navy vessels as we could.

I'd gone to see Lieutenant Warwick first thing that morning, and it had not been difficult to persuade him to help us, for it was not his belief that ordinary men should be pressed into service. When he heard first

Will's story, then the circumstances which had caused Betsy and me to be on board, he said he felt we had been treated unjustly and it was his duty, not as an officer but as a gentleman, to aid us. In turn I assured him most sincerely that I would inform Lord and Lady Baysmith of his noble behaviour towards us, and do everything in my power to advance his suit with Miss Sophia.

'I am certain that she still loves you, sir,' I said. 'In my experience of young ladies, the more their parents oppose their wishes, the more they cling to them.'

'And she refused to be introduced to the gentleman in Bath, you said?'

'She did, sir!' I replied.

He thought for a moment. 'We are stopping in Madeira; perhaps you could beg Sophia to contact me care of the Royal Navy office there. I can send her a list of the stops the ship is making and we can write to one another at each one.'

'Of course, sir,' I said fervently. 'I will tell her everything that happened, and assure her of your complete devotion.'

'I'll try to get passage on a fast ship back from Australia. It'll be eighteen months, Kitty – please make Sophia aware of this.'

'Indeed I will, sir.' I took a deep breath. 'But about Will, and me, and Betsy . . .'

'Yes!' He seemed to pull himself from his reverie. 'Sadly, Annie Lease, one of the two girls who were ill, has died, so I have already ordered a sea burial this afternoon. The Plymouth authorities won't think of taking the body ashore; they're too frightened that gaol fever will come in with the corpse.'

'But won't they . . .' I hesitated, for it sounded so callous, '. . . want to wait in case the other girl dies so they can bury them together?'

'What – set sail on a long voyage with a dead body on board?' He shook his head. 'Never! Sailors are a super-stitious bunch.' He was quiet for a moment, then said, 'No, you will be in the other canvas shroud, playing dead. And it will be me who sews you in, so you can rest easy that I won't do the final stitch.'

I looked at him curiously.

'In a shipboard burial,' he explained, 'when the body is stitched into its canvas wrap it's usual to put the last stitch through the corpse's nose to make sure it's dead.'

I shuddered.

'And Will, of course, will be our boatman,' he contin-ued.

'But what of Betsy?'

'She can be in your canvas with you.' He frowned slightly. 'Though you'll have the awkward responsibility of explaining to her what you're doing.'

'I'll try and think of something,' I said, my mind skit-tering all over the place.

Lieutenant Warwick told me that the burial was to be at five o'clock that afternoon and that Betsy and I should be in the infirmary at four o'clock. He then went off to make the necessary arrangements.

Finding Betsy, I took her off to the quietest corner I could find, well away from the distraction of the livestock. Sitting down on the deck beside her, I looked her over carefully, wondering how much she'd been affected by the things she'd been through and how she'd deal with the part which was coming next. Her little face was scaly with salt, there were what looked like cold sores around her mouth and, though she was bundled up in shawls, her fingers were chapped with cold. She also had chilblains on her toes, because I'd had to cut off the tips of her shoes to enable her to fit into them. She looked poor and neglected, though I didn't know how I could have done more for her.

'Betsy,' I whispered, 'what if someone was to give you a wish . . .'

'Like in Cinderella?' she asked straight away, because Margaret told all the children stories at night.

I nodded.

'Then I would have mice turned into horses and a sparkly gown to go to the ball.'

'Yes,' I said, 'that's what Cinderella wanted. But if you got a wish, what do you think you'd wish for?'

She thought for a long moment. 'I'd wish for Will.'

'Ah.' I let my breath out in a sigh. 'Now, what if I found a way to make that wish come true?'

She stared at me. 'Like a fairy godmother?'

'A little bit like a fairy godmother. I think I might be able to grant your wish, but you'll have to do something for me first.'

'Is it to go to sleep for a hundred years?'

I laughed, because it was something along those lines. 'That's Sleeping Beauty. No, I don't want you to sleep for a hundred years, just for a little while. And you have to *pretend* to be asleep, that's all.'

She nodded. 'All right. Can I go and see the animals now?'

'Yes, you can. But when I call you, you must come straight away and do everything I tell you.' I took her hands. 'Everything, mind,' I said with careful emphasis, 'even if it seems very strange. And if you do what I say, then your wish will come true and when you wake up, you'll see Will.'

Her face lit up.

'Do you understand?'

She nodded solemnly.

'And, Betsy, you mustn't tell anyone. Even Robyn.'

'Is it a special secret?'

'Yes, it is.'

'Now can I go?'

'Yes, you can,' I said, and she sped off.

I don't remember how I spent those last hours on board, just that I was in an agony of suspense. I suspected everyone who boarded of knowing our intentions; every shout from a sailor and every command from an officer made my heart leap with fright. There was one terrible moment when an official from the courts in London arrived with a scroll under his arm and I felt certain it was something to do with me and I was going to be hauled back to Newgate. It was a reprieve, however, for Verity, a girl of fifteen who'd been found guilty of the theft from her mistress of an emerald necklace. With just hours to go before the ship sailed, her mistress had remembered that she'd lent the necklace to a friend.

I hid myself away most of that day, not wanting to be the least bit conspicuous. I told Martha to make up some tale to reassure Robyn about our disappearance and said that she could, later and in confidence, also tell Margaret. As for the others – well, there were so many of us now crowded into the airless, muggy orlop at night, fighting over our bread allowance, bickering over some slight or other, that even if ten girls disappeared it would hardly be remarked upon. I heard one girl saying that, with luck, a few more would die and leave better rations for the rest.

At the due time I bid a tearful goodbye to Martha and gave her my address at Bridgeford Hall so that, in all hopefulness, we might be in contact again at some point in the future. I could not take anything with me, so I gave her my second-best dress and a few little things that I'd collected, which she was pleased with. After that, I found Betsy as planned, and together we went to the infirmary.

Chapter Twenty-Seven

🌸

The rowing boat rocked. The canvas was clammy and heavy about me, and I felt sick and disorientated. My idea of hell, I now knew, was to be consigned for ever to the bottom of a boat in the bitterest of weathers, being joggled first one way, then the next, never seeing daylight or knowing when I'd be released. I did not relish either being in such close proximity to the corpse of Annie Lease, and was trying to keep my mind off this matter.

'I think we are far enough away from the ship,' I heard Lieutenant Warwick say at last. 'Heave to, sailor!'

I heard a creak and a splash as the oars changed direction and Betsy wriggled against me, her hair in my nostrils smelling like damp, dirty straw.

'Can I talk now? Can I move?' she whispered.

'In just a moment,' I whispered back.

I was excited and a little apprehensive, wondering how Betsy would react on seeing Will. She had no idea that it was he who was rowing us to freedom; he'd only arrived after we'd been placed in our canvas shroud and prayed over by the chaplain.

'Allow me to release you,' came Lieutenant Warwick's voice, and I heard the sound of canvas being sliced open by a penknife. It fell away and there he was, immaculate in full dress uniform, smiling at both of us. 'What a good and well behaved child you are,' he said, lifting Betsy from me.

Betsy rubbed her eyes, confused, for when we'd climbed into our canvas coffin it had been dusk. Now it was dark and the only light came from the lantern swinging on the yardarm, and the moon appearing out of the clouds now and then. She looked around.

'Where's my brother? You said he –' she began, and then she spotted Will and burst into tears. After the tears came a few moments of aloof disdain when she wouldn't even look at him, then a little display of temper, and finally a hurried clambering across the boat to be held tightly in his arms.

After that it was my turn to be held so – and following that there was such an amount of laughing and crying in the small boat, it was as though Betsy and I really had come back from the dead.

We were brought back to reality by a gentlemanly cough from Lieutenant Warwick, who said he had to return to the ship. Will therefore took his penknife and sprung open first his leg irons, then mine, and we threw them overboard.

'I have a rough map of the Sound,' Will said, and he loosened Betsy's hands around him and delved into his oilskin cape to consult a square of paper. 'If it's convenient to you, sir, I'll row us towards the green which leads to the turnpike road, where you can leave us.'

Lieutenant Warwick nodded. 'Before that, let us not forget our other duty,' he said and, bidding Will take up one end of the canvas-wrapped bundle containing Annie Lease, they slipped it into the sea. It sank straight away, for it was weighted with stones. As it did so I said a little prayer for the girl who'd unwittingly helped our escape – and prayed for myself, too, that I'd never have to go to sea in any sort of a boat ever again.

The lieutenant and Will rolled up the canvas that Betsy and I had been concealed in, and this was also thrown into the sea and, being similarly weighted, it slipped under the water. Will then began rowing powerfully to where the lights of the land flickered. I stared at him in the gloom: at his outline, his strong arms on the oars, his straight back, his pigtail of hair shiny with grease. Oh thank the Lord that we had found each other again!

On reaching land, Will beached the rowing boat on a spit of sand and the three of us got out, leaving Lieutenant Warwick to return to the *Juanita*. He said farewell to each of us in turn, shaking hands with Will, kissing Betsy's head, and patting my shoulder in an awkward manner, and I could not find words enough to thank him for what he had done for us. I wished then that I could be like my young

Misses, educated in the art of making pretty speeches, but all I could do was stutter a few words and turn away, my eyes brimming with tears.

It was our fervent hope that, in the chaos of getting the ship ready to sail, Will would not be missed, but in case it was seen that Lieutenant Warwick had come back on his own, he was going to say there had been a struggle to gain control of the rowing boat and Will had fallen overboard and drowned. The pressed men, Will had already told me, were the very lowliest members of the ship's crew, hardly regarded as crew at all and, as with the cargo of girls, one more or less made little difference to anyone.

The three of us sat on the grass for a while until the lieutenant's boat disappeared between the numerous other craft. It might have been a romantic moment, for we were free of all constraints, the stars were glittering and the moon was sailing like a silver disc in the clear sky – but what happened next was that I was violently sick and had to tear a strip of fabric from the hem of my gown in order to cleanse myself. I felt wretched, tired and nauseous, and – Betsy now being half asleep – Will said we should try and find shelter under a hedge or in a barn and start our walk home the following day. Saying this, he looked up to the sky and pointed out some significant stars, telling me that he'd learned a little navi-gation from the sailors. We needed to travel north, apparently, towards the Pole Star, in order to reach Bridge-ford, which he thought was some twenty miles off.

We set off and I enjoyed the freedom of being unshackled, although before we'd gone very far I was overcome with exhaustion and felt that, despite the harshness of the weather, I could have slept soundly in the middle of a turnip field. Seeing my great tiredness, Will went a little way ahead, Betsy on his shoulder, to spy out the countryside. He came back to say that he'd located a barn. This proved to be somewhat dilapidated, two of its walls having fallen out, but was well provided with soft hay. We scooped out nests within and fell asleep immediately.

At first light the next morning we started off again, all very hungry, and were happy to discover we had just enough money between us to buy a crusty cottage loaf and some cheese from a farmhouse. We ate this as we walked and enjoyed our meal immensely. It was a fresh, crisp morning, the sky was a vivid blue, and the sun was skittering in and out between puffy clouds.

When Betsy was occupied calling up to squirrels or counting the cows in faraway fields, Will and I spoke at length about what sort of reception we might get at Bridgeford Hall. I longed to be there, but was very apprehensive in case my story might not be believed, and Will was concerned that he would be held responsible for abandoning Betsy.

'And if someone's stolen my boat or taken over my job and hut, what will I do for a living?' His face suddenly paled. 'What if a press gang come for me again? If it's found out that I've jumped ship I'll face the death penalty for sure.'

I stopped walking and looked at him consideringly. 'You must disguise yourself,' I said. 'You must stop wearing that pigtail and discard the kerchief.' I put out my hand and gently touched the new scar on his lip. 'Perhaps you should grow a beard to hide that.'

He caught hold of my hand, held it to his lips and kissed it, and we were transfixed for a moment, staring at each other, until Betsy turned and saw us and, running up, laughingly tried to pull us apart.

'So, Betsy, Kitty thinks I should put on a disguise and grow a beard!' Will said.

'And he must have a new name, too! What can you think of?' I asked Betsy, and she started to invent many strange and absurd names which kept us laughing as we passed through several more villages.

'How much longer until we get home?' Betsy now began asking at every corner, every stile, every field, and was maintaining a thin and continuous whine between times. Will began piggybacking her, then carried her in his arms, and I took a turn but couldn't carry her for long.

'Shall we stop and sleep a while?' I asked, for I felt very weary, but Will shook his head and said we must try to get back by nightfall, for there were signs there would be a very hard frost and he didn't think it was wise to expose Betsy to it.

We carried on and tried to get a lift on a farm cart, but

the first two we stopped weren't going in the right direction. The next one slowed right down, making us hopeful, but its driver looked us over then flicked his whip for the horse to trot on.

I knew I must look terrible, for it had been some time since I'd washed myself properly, and I could not remember when I'd last pulled a comb through my hair. My gown was stained and torn, my face and hands grimy, my feet bloody through chilblains and blisters – and Betsy looked like the most neglected of street urchins.

Will, as disappointed as I, said nothing, but moved Betsy to his other shoulder. We walked on, choosing our way by the direction of the watery sun and by the milestones at the sides of the roads.

The closer we came the more I felt apprehensive about the welcome we might receive when we arrived. Lord Baysmith was known to be a strict authoritarian: how would he feel about harbouring an escaped criminal under his roof? Suppose Mrs Bonny preferred Patience as a milkmaid and didn't wish to employ me any longer, or Miss Alice didn't believe my tale of robbery and called the constables?

We did not approach Bridgeford by way of the river, but went over the bridge in Thorndyke, Will saying that he would accompany me to the hall first to help me tell my story, then go down to the river and see how it stood with his boat and hut.

When, at last, the gravelled drive of Bridgeford Hall came into view, I felt almost as sick and terrified as I'd done on entering Newgate. A bunch of five or six children I recognised as belonging to the estate workers were playing on the wrought-iron gate, swinging it to and fro, and as we passed through they stared at us open-mouthed.

Betsy struggled to get out of Will's arms. 'It's *me*!' she said, jumping up and down in front of them. 'I've been to London and been in a prison and been in a ship and gone to Australia!'

Despite my anxiety I managed to smile, but the children, looking dumbfounded, ran helter-skelter back along the drive towards the house and disappeared through the side door.

Will and I exchanged glances. 'Do I look *very* disreputable?' he asked.

'Yes,' I said. 'Do I?'

'Worse than ever,' he said, but his eyes smiled into mine most tenderly.

Seeing that the chippings on the driveway were hurting Betsy's toes, Will stopped to lift her up on to his shoulders again. He and I then walked together towards Bridgeford Hall, both of us too overwrought to say a word.

When we were twenty yards away from the hall a surprising thing happened: the kitchen door crashed open and all the children ran out of the house, swiftly followed by Mrs Bonny, wiping her hands on her apron, and Mr Griffin just seconds behind her. Prudence and Patience came next, and then, from down the front steps of the hall ran Christina, Miss Sophia's maid, followed by Miss Alice and Miss Sophia themselves, both looking startled but elegant in different shades of blue velvet. All stood thus, smiling and waiting for us. As we drew near Mrs Bonny began clapping and then held out her arms, and Mr Griffin waved, and the others cheered and called, 'Welcome home!'

I looked at Will, and he looked at me. We would both have to tell our stories, of course, but it seemed, by all that was wonderful, that we were still wanted at the house.

We glanced at each other, linked our hands together tightly, and then stepped through the door into the welcoming warmth of Bridgeford Hall.

What Happened Next

The whole family – even Lord Baysmith – were called in to hear Kitty and Will's story, and the young couple were embarrassed to find themselves the centre of attention for several days. Kitty's story seemed barely credible, but it so happened that the landlady of the guest house where Kitty had been due to stay was so worried when her guest failed to arrive that she wrote to Miss Alice to inform her. The letter also mentioned that there had been a spate of robberies in the Charing Cross area, the thieves targeting those newly arrived in the city. As regards to the ship, Lord Baysmith had heard of the *Juanita* and her cargo of women, so Kitty's story was believed absolutely and everyone at Bridgeford Hall vowed to say that, if a police constable should enquire, she had never even been to London. Luckily Miss Alice had managed to obtain a copy of *Pride and Prejudice* from her literary gentleman friend.

The letter that Kitty sent from gaol never reached her parents so, having been told by Mrs Bonny that she hadn't returned to the hall, they were thrilled to know that she was safe and well, and Kitty was given two days off to visit them.

Patience had not proved a great success with the cows, who, whether milked by her or one of the cowhands, were not giving the yield that they had with Kitty. Mrs Bonny was only too pleased, therefore, to give Kitty her old job back in the dairy.

No Navy men came looking for Will, and at the end of the Napoleonic Wars in 1815 the practice of pressing men into service was outlawed. As a result of his experiences, however, he had lost the urge to go to work in London. Sadly, Will's boat had been stolen in his absence, but Lord Baysmith was so moved by the story of what he had been through that he lent him the money to buy a new one. Lord Baysmith also sent some of the estate workers down to make improvements to Will's hut on the riverbank, though it was understood that Kitty hoped for something more substantial on their marriage.

Kitty spent a lot of time deep in private conversations with Miss Sophia and Miss Alice, speaking about Lieutenant Warwick, and there was much weeping and running up and down the stairs during this period. Between them, the three girls were able to convince Lord and Lady Baysmith that Lieutenant Warwick was a very decent fellow and worthy of Miss Sophia's love. Miss Sophia was permitted to write to him care of his ship, her letter being despatched swiftly by a Russian steamship to await the arrival of the *Juanita* in Cape Town. Their mutual fondness being restored, the romance between them blossomed.

Will's sister, Kate, and her family returned to the village in the spring. On George showing great contrition, Mr Cox allowed them to move back into their old cottage. Kate – who was feeling very guilty at ever having left her – took Betsy back into their household, but Betsy always spent the summer by the river with Will.

And as for Kitty and her ferryman, one very fine May morning, when the meadow buttercups were just beginning to reveal their yellow faces to the sun, they made their wedding vows, and Mr and Mrs Villiers stepped over the threshold of their new home.

Some Historical Notes from the Author

Pride and Prejudice

Jane Austen's novels were published in the Regency period, during which George III was declared insane and his son appointed Prince Regent.

Pride and Prejudice is now considered a literary masterpiece, and is widely known across the world through numerous television and film adaptations too.

But it was not always so. *Pride and Prejudice* began its life in 1796 with the title *First Impressions* and, turned down by the bookseller to whom it was offered, was renamed, rewritten several times and eventually sold for just £110. In January 1813 it was published in three hardcover volumes by Thomas Egerton of Whitehall, London, priced at 18 shillings. Its author was named merely as 'A Lady', and there was much speculation as to who this lady might be.

It is thought that only 700 copies were printed but, due to several favourable reviews and acclaim from

Britain's reading public (a much smaller, more elite group than today, of course), it sold out and was reprinted in November that same year.

The author died in 1817 and during the 1820s her work went through a period of obscurity when her books were out of print and she was hardly talked about. In 1833, *Pride and Prejudice*, along with several other of her novels, came out in a cheaper edition, and this helped to make her more widely known. When the copyright of *Pride and Prejudice* expired in 1841, however, there was no rush by other publishers to obtain the text.

Jane Austen's fame gradually increased, and now *Pride and Prejudice* consistently reaches the top three in votes for 'Britain's favourite book'.

Newgate Prison

The first prison on the Newgate site was built in 1188. It burned down several times over the years, including in the Great Fire of London in 1666. Conditions were either bad or terrible, depending on how much money you had to help you pay your way through prison. Women were allowed to take their dependant children into gaol with them, and there were several tragic cases of women being taken to the scaffold with their babies in their arms.

Public executions were held outside the prison until 1868 and always drew large crowds, especially if the person being hanged was popular with the people. It was usual, with a popular criminal, to exhibit his or her clothes and effects, sometimes with an accompanying coffin, in one of the London taverns.

A major problem with both Newgate and the other London prisons was overcrowding, but the Royal Navy produced a regular flow of *hulks* – decommissioned ships too battered and no longer seaworthy enough to be used in combat, but ideal for housing the overflow of prisoners. Sited on the Medway and the Thames, they were often used as holding bays for those prisoners who were awaiting transportation.

Early in the nineteenth century, the Quaker reformer Elizabeth Fry became very concerned about the conditions in which female prisoners and their children lived. She lobbied Parliament, formed education classes and supplied clothes to women in prison, hoping to increase their self-esteem. Despite her intervention, it wasn't until 1858 that the interior of Newgate was improved, remodelled and formed into individual cells, thus enabling prisoners a little more privacy.

The prison was demolished in 1904. The Central Criminal Court, also known as the Old Bailey, now stands on the site.

All the information about Newgate has been taken from books on the topic (see *Bibliography*) and research of various records in the Guildhall Library. The crimes committed and spoken of by the girls Kitty met in prison are based on real cases.

The Law

During the Regency period the law was harsh, there were no proper provisions for the poor and many offences carried the death penalty.

The Bow Street Runners, set up in the 1740s and so called because they operated from Bow Street in Covent Garden, were one of the earliest groups of thief-takers, hired by the Bow Street magistrates' office to apprehend felons. This, the authorities hoped, would make it more likely that criminals would be caught and so deter them from committing crimes in the first place.

By the end of the eighteenth century, London had seven police centres and a substantial body of watchmen employed to prevent and detect crime. In 1829 the Metropolitan Police was formed – a centralised force of some 3,000 men under the control of the home secretary.

Most of the information on the law and criminal trials was taken from the records at www.oldbaileyonline.org.

Transportation

English gaols – and especially London gaols – were always fearfully overcrowded, and to be exiled to another country was a common punishment for both major and minor crimes from the early 1600s until 1868. British criminals were deported to the United States until the 1770s, but following the American War of Independence, the authorities began to send them to Australia. It was seen as a useful and humane alternative to execution, which probably would have been the sentence of many if transportation had not been introduced.

A sentence could be for life or for a minimum of seven years, and convicts would typically be expected to work in the colonies by farming, mining or building roads. When they had served their sentence – or most of their sentence – they would be granted certain freedoms: to marry and raise a family, and to work and live where they pleased. In the unlikely event that they could raise the fare, they were free to return to England.

Throughout the eighteenth century, women and their children were often amongst the prisoners deported to Australia, but were in the minority, until 1789, when approximately 230 women and children were sent to Botany Bay aboard a ship called the *Lady Julian*. Some of these women were prostitutes, while others had been convicted of quite minor crimes, but their main reason for being transported was to enable them to marry male prisoners already living in Australia and thereby increase the population. If the women were over childbearing age they were made to do the tedious sorts of jobs usually done by those in workhouses.

First, though, was the year-long journey to Australia, during which the women were encouraged to 'become friendly' with the sailors. In *The Floating Brothel*, a fascinating account of the *Lady Julian*'s voyage, Sian Rees tells how each shipmate was encouraged to choose a woman for the duration of the voyage and sets of baby clothes were part of the ship's provisions. How the women felt about this, and whether they had any choice in the shipmates' selection, is not recorded.

May Revels

Until very recently – and, who knows, maybe it still goes on – the innocent tradition of washing one's face in the dew of a May morning was thought to be excellent for the skin and to bring beauty and good health. The diarist Samuel Pepys, writing 350 years ago (and 150 years before *The Disgrace of Kitty Grey* is set), records that he was woken at three o'clock in the morning by his wife going out in a coach with her maids to gather May dew.

There are many other traditions connected with the month of May. The chief of these, perhaps, is maypole dancing, which was stopped by the Puritans during the Civil War because it was believed to encourage free and easy behaviour amongst the young. Nowadays a much more sedate version can be seen on our village greens and playgrounds, when schoolchildren dance around a pole with ribbons.

In Helston, Cornwall, the traditional Furry Dance, the Flora, still goes on. On a particular day in May, the streets are decorated with bunting and greenery, and men and women in their best Sunday outfits dance through the streets, going in and out of the houses and shops.

Morris men have long been a popular form of entertainment for May Day and summer. Usually these dances are performed by men, the dancers wearing traditional costume enlivened by colourful flowers, ribbons, sashes and bells. Two teams dance together and around each other, each side consisting of six dancers, a fool and sometimes a hobby horse.

Other parts of the country put on pageants and plays in May, or have decorated horses and carts going around the streets with floats depicting various aspects of country life. The final cart in these processions usually features the May Queen: a young local girl dressed in white, crowned with blossom and attended by flower girls. In some areas of the country she might be joined by a boy playing the part of Jack o' the Green. *Tableaux vivants* were also popular forms of entertainment, sometimes presented on a theatre stage, on a cart pulled by a shire horse or in an aristocratic drawing room.

Town and Country Dairies

In times gone by, many families in the country would have kept a cow of their own to ensure that they were supplied with milk, butter and cheese throughout the year. When, from the eighteenth century onwards, the common grazing land began to be enclosed and taken over by the big landowners, families were forced to get rid of their cows. Consequently they had to buy their milk and butter from their local estate owner, who usually grew very rich.

I imagined that a particular landowner, Lord Baysmith, had not only a thriving dairy business of his own, but a 'model dairy' to supply dairy products to his household. Gentleman farmers and estate owners often showed a great enthusiasm for dairying, building spotlessly clean dairies, usually on the north wall of a house and under the shade of trees so it would stay as cool as possible.

In London it was slightly different! Sometimes cows were kept in tiny cowsheds, often below ground and in appalling conditions, with no access to fresh air nor pasture nor space for the thorough cleaning of the animals. Milk could also be purchased straight from the cows in the various London parks, so you might have been better off taking along your own jug to be filled there rather than relying on the milkman. Not all dairies were as bad as Mr Holloway's, and at one time there really was a beautifully tiled dairy on the Strand called Nell Gwyn's Dairy.

The proliferation of cows and other animals (pigs, sheep, chickens) in this 'backyard agriculture' added to the piles of filth left in stalls and carried away by the night-soil men or, more usually, deposited in kennels in the street, then washed down by rain and swept into the Thames. And it was the Thames which supplied most of London's drinking water, of course.

An Old-fashioned Method for Making Butter

The milk to be used for making the butter should not be cooled but poured into a setting dish and left overnight.

The next morning the cream, which will have risen to the top, should be skimmed off, covered with muslin and left for 48 hours to ripen.

The next stage is the churning. The inside of the churn is washed out with salt water before being filled with the cream. The churning is normally done by means of a plunger, which is moved up and down at high speed until, eventually, the butter is formed. A dairy-maid could also use something called a 'rocker churn', which is pushed backwards and forwards like a baby's cradle, or a 'box churn' with a handle, which revolves paddles to turn the cream. Sometimes glass butter-jars are used for making small amounts of butter.

Constant inspection is necessary to ensure that the butter is not over-churned, as this will impair the separation of the whey. Only when the butter has come together and looks perfectly sound should the watery mixture, called whey, be drained off. This can be used in cooking later or given to the pigs.

The butter should then be washed in cold water and transferred to a butter-worker (a device for removing excess moisture). After this, it should be spread in a trough and a roller device moved up and down over it, thus squeezing out any extra whey.

The butter should then be removed with big wooden

butter-pats to a hard surface and quickly worked into the desired shape: an oblong or a cylinder. The finished shapes can be decorated with stamps bearing a floral design, or perhaps impressed with the coat of arms of the estate owner.

Bibliography

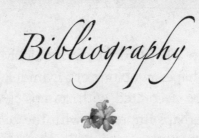

Ackroyd, Peter, *London – The Biography*, Vintage, 2000

Day, Malcolm, *Voices from the World of Jane Austen*, David & Charles, 2006

Downing, Sarah Jane, *Fashion in the Time of Jane Austen*, Shire Publications, 2010

Grovier, Kelly, *The Gaol – The Story of Newgate, London's Most Notorious Prison*, John Murray, 2008

Gulvin, K.R., *The Medway Prison Hulks*, L13 Light Industrial Workshop, 2010

Halliday, Stephen, *Newgate – London's Prototype of Hell*, The History Press, 2009

Harman, Claire, *Jane's Fame – How Jane Austen Conquered the World*, Canongate Books, 2009

Rees, Sian, *The Floating Brothel*, Hodder, 2001

White, Jerry, *London in the Nineteenth Century*, Vintage, 2007